TH
GOVERNESS

PHOEBE GARDENER

Safe Sex is essential: your very life may depend on it. Please remember that some of the sexual practices that are featured in this work of fiction (written in an era that pre-dates lethal STDs) are dangerous and they are not recommended or in any way endorsed by the publishers; by the same token, we do not condone any form of non-consensual sex for any reason: it is reprehensible and illegal and should never become a part of a person's real life: rather it should remain firmly in the realm of sexual fantasy.

The Young Governess
Past Venus Historical
London 2006

Past Venus Historical

is an imprint of

THE *Erotic* Print Society

EPS, 1st Floor, 17 Harwood Road,

LONDON SW6 4QP

Tel: 0800 026 25 24

Email: eros@eroticprints.org

Web: www.eroticprints.org

© 2006 MacHo Ltd, London UK

ISBN : 1-904989-19-5

Printed and bound in Spain by BookPrint S.L., Barcelona

No part of this publication may be reproduced by any means without the express written permission of the Publishers. The moral right of the author of the text and the artists has been asserted.

While every effort has been made by PVH to contact copyright holders it may not have been possible to get in touch with certain publishers or authors of former editions of some of the titles published in this series.

THE YOUNG GOVERNESS

PHOEBE GARDENER

*E*PS

Chapter One

As the train pulled into Windsor station, Katherine Spencer could not resist giving in to a girlish impulse. She lowered the window down a couple of notches on the broad leather strap so that, by craning her neck only a little, she could lean out (taking care not to touch the grimy brass sill) and enjoy a fine panorama of the platform's busy throng as it glided past. The scene did not disappoint her. There were travellers of all shapes and sizes, porters, guards, and plenty, it seemed, from that curious class of person that inhabited stations for no obviously good reason, the loafer. The train slowed to a halt and, amid clouds of steam and acrid coal smoke that billowed up to the glass and iron roof, the very air seemed to shake with the repeated slammings of heavy carriage doors as passengers stepped down from the train and, gathering up their luggage or seeking a porter, made their way towards the ticket gate. To most this noxious blend of steam and smoke was no more than the necessary stench of modern transport, but to Kate it was the sweet smell of liberty, yet another confirmation that her dearest hopes and aspirations were well on their way to becoming realised.

When she herself alighted it was with the purest thrill she thought that here, on this very platform, the Queen's dainty feet had also trod, albeit on a fine red carpet reserved for the occasion.

"Fetch yer luggage down, Miss?"

Kate smiled graciously at the florid-faced porter who seemed to have materialised from nowhere, and she pointed to her luggage on the rack with a gloved finger. It was a warm June day, and the porter's male sweat caused Kate's nose to wrinkle slightly as he emerged from the compartment with her valises and heavy portmanteau and proceeded to load them on to his barrow.

As Kate, the porter and her luggage weaved through the crowd towards the exit, her impassive demeanour gave away little of her inner thoughts; in fact her mind was in turmoil, oscillating between the irrational anxieties of the unseasoned traveller and the heady excitement of a grand adventure.

Handing her ticket in at the barrier, she started to rummage for her purse in the pocket of her light travelling cloak, but a tall, elegantly liveried coachman stepped in between Kate and companion and said, "Miss Spencer? I'll take care of that, Ma'am," smoothly slipping the perspiring, expectant porter a reward that seemed to be, judging from his gap-toothed grin, on the generous side of adequate. She looked from one man to the other. Her rescuer was handsome, she thought, clean-limbed, blue-eyed and square-jawed. Mentally, she chastised herself for this rather too nice observation. Handsome young coachmen were all very well, but it did a young lady no good at all to assess their physical attributes in such a way when she was the first to admit that she aspired to more suitable male company.

Kate followed her rescuer to his carriage, where a similarly attired, older man stood by the horses. As they arrived, the second coachman gave her a little salute by raising his fingers to the gold cockade of his black top hat. He bent down to release the landau's steps while his partner secured the luggage. Kate placed her small, neatly booted foot on the lowest rung and climbed gracefully into the carriage. She had time to glance at the discreet coat of arms on the shiny black lacquered door and, once seated, she could also appreciate the gleaming brass work and the immaculate leather and cloth upholstery. The carriage, its coachmen and its occupant moved off at a gentle trot down Windsor High Street, eliciting the occasional curious glance of a passer-by; Kate settled back to enjoy the ride; she felt almost as grand as the Queen herself. She glanced up at the Castle walls on one side and the smart shop fronts on the other. Crossing the Thames at Windsor Bridge she looked down upon the flurry of boating activity on the river where every sort of river craft, from humble skiff to elegant steam launch, seemed to be out that day.

Soon they left the busy hum of town far behind and as they followed the meandering road through lush meadows and fields of green corn, Kate had time to loosen the bow of her bonnet, tilt her head back on the plush seat and reflect on the unhappy circumstances that had thrust her into this entirely new episode of her relatively short life.

Upon his death, her long-ailing and beloved Papa had left Kate all but destitute – and an orphan, so to speak – since her mother had died when Kate was a child. It had been two years ago, only weeks after her twenty-first birthday, and at first Kate was inconsolable, but she had been fortunate enough to be taken under the wing of a neighbouring family. Her neighbours, the local magistrate and his wife, had been kind towards her. As the highly educated daughter of a retired schoolmaster, she had been able to tutor their two young children in return for bed and board. George Belfont had recognised both a spark of ambition and a streak of determination in their young guest, and as soon as her period of mourning was over, he had quietly reminded her of the choices of career that her none-too-promising wealth and status of an impoverished, genteel spinster accorded her: village school teacher, lady's companion or governess. He pointed out that the latter seemed to offer the most direct path towards a fourth, and certainly more desirable, career for a pretty, intelligent and competent young woman: that of matrimony.

* * *

Marriage was certainly something of an ambition for the pretty young governess. And this ambition had come about in a rather unorthodox way. As an only child whose mother had departed this life shortly after Kate's second birthday and whose father, though a loving and conscientious parent, was more often than not preoccupied by his work, she was much given to wandering the streams, fields and hedgerows that surrounded their village. Especially fascinating to her was a patch of common woodland, with dense and almost impenetrable undergrowth. A keen naturalist and budding ornithologist, young Kate would often set off across the fields to this location in order to bring back specimens of natural history to show her father or, if he were busy, their housekeeper, Mrs Proctor.

This kindly, intelligent, widow had looked after her for the past ten years and was more substitute mother than servant to Kate, more elder sister than housekeeper. Her knowledge of country lore was considerable, and she was always happy to help Kate identify the specimens she returned with.

One summer's afternoon, a little before Kate's sixteenth birthday, she found herself in the small space formed by the junction of two hedgerows, an almost cave-like bower; she had come to look at a blackbird's nest she had discovered the previous day, to see if the bird was still sitting. Just as she found the four greenish blue, brown-speckled eggs, she heard laughter and voices. She immediately recognised them as belonging to Joss Witherspoon and the butcher's daughter, Rosie Jebb, a pretty lass, whose curly golden tresses possessed a hint of red that complimented her creamy, freckled complexion to perfection. She was a wild, spirited girl, only a couple of years older than Kate and had a reputation of being 'fast' with boys, although were she to be truthful, Kate wasn't really sure what this meant. And Joss, with his dark, gypsy looks, who sometimes came to tend their garden, was a respectful, pleasant enough lad, always dressed in a patched, ragged jacket, breeches tied with twine, his collarless shirt sometimes open so that Kate had once seen the way that the dark hair on his chest went all the way down to his navel. She wasn't certain why, but this had given her a guilty little thrill of excitement. Now, peering from her hidden shelter, she could see that both Rosie and Joss's clothes were loose and open: Joss holding his trousers up having undone the twine belt that held it up and Rosie's pale, pink-tipped breasts bursting out from the tight confines of her unbuttoned russet dress.

"Are you going to do me here, then, Joss?"

Rosie's voice had a gently mocking lilt to it.

"Reckon I will, Rosie. Here's as good a place as any."

There was a sound of the tall grass being beaten down into a makeshift bed.

"Come on now, off with yer dress, and down with yer drawers, there's a good girl." And there was laughter in his voice, too.

To her mortification, Kate realised that not only were they within a couple of feet of her secret bower, but they had blocked its exit, too, and she had no way of leaving without declaring herself. She was trapped! She would have to stay until they had finished whatever it was they were going to do. And what were they going to do? 'Off with her dress and down with her drawers?' Was Rosie about to answer the call of nature in front of Joss? She most certainly hoped not – it would be too embarrassing for words! Now she could see Rosie, as she stood facing her hiding place.

With hands on hips, head lowered and brow knitted in a mock-serious frown, Rosie gave her taller companion a playful look through long, fair eyelashes as an unruly strand of golden hair fell across her brow.

"Reckon I'll be doing that for you, Joss," she answered, tossing her head and blowing the strand off her face, and then followed on more sternly, "but you'll have to kiss me again first. And kiss and squeeze my titties. I likes that. And I likes it better still when you kiss my cunt, and all."

Spooning! Kissing! So that's what it was all about. Kate smiled to herself for she had seen courting couples come this way, arm in arm, stealing kisses when they thought no one was looking, but she was puzzled, too, she had never heard the word 'cunt' before and she wondered what it meant.

"Now let's see that fine John Thomas of yours. I'll give it a suck, if you like, here... Oh, that's nice, that is... I wants that inside me I do... but don't you dare forget now, to pull out and spend on my belly. And don't you do that until I've had a chance to spend meself!" and she giggled in a way that Kate thought was quite foolish for a grown girl.

Kate, quite hidden, was beside herself with frustration and curiosity. None of what she now heard made any sense to her. They had shifted again, and Joss – tall, good-looking, dark Joss – stood with his back to her, clad only in his shirt now, feet planted wide apart, while Rosie knelt in the flattened grass in front of him and was doing something she could not see.

Hardly daring to breathe, she moved her position silently so that she could see through another little chink in the thicket. Rosie had dispensed with her dress and undergarments and knelt in front of young Joss entirely nude: her breasts, belly and her sex, were all exposed to the more innocent girl's spellbound gaze. She was so hairy down there, thought Kate. Not like my downy little patch, but a great reddish-gold bush with her blushing nether-lips showing so clearly, all swollen and pouting. But what made Kate's eyes widen in pure amazement was the long fleshy stalk that sprouted from the tangle of black hair at the base of Master Witherspoon's flat belly. It was as thick and as long as the biggest pork sausages that Rosie's father sold in his butcher's shop... and... why Rosie had the end of it in her *mouth!* As if she were actually *sucking* it... so, of *course*, this must be Joss's 'John Thomas' that Rosie had talked of!

Kate had felt alarmed, excited, and

somehow not a little grown-up to be witnessing all this. But what came next caused an entirely different group of emotions to flow through her already confused young mind. After only a few minutes, Joss pushed Rosie down onto the bed of grass and Kate could see that Rosie's fingers were parting the petals of her sex and that – oh *no!* – Joss had lowered his head between her thighs until he was... *kissing* her down there! Kate could clearly hear the liquid sounds that his tongue was making as he licked and lapped her for a few moments more, Rosie giving loud moans of pleasure. There was a further change of positions and now Rosie's lover was placing the purple, bell-shaped end of his 'John Thomas' – now grown even larger and stiffer - into that tender part of her anatomy, and with a great thrust of his loins, drove it in to its very roots. Rosie gave a great shriek and Kate winced in sympathy for the poor girl who was obviously horribly injured by violence that this callous youth had done to her.

It seemed there was to be no end to the number of surprises given to Kate that day; far from continuing to scream in pain, a look of pure rapture transformed the older girl's features. And, while he thrust and thrust like a madman, Rosie would caress Joss's head and mutter endearments to him in a sweet tone of voice. Far from hurt, what she was experiencing was obviously the greatest of pleasures as she alternated her wails of passion (for now Kate recognised them as such) with strange uncouth-sounding grunts and exhortations that meant little to her unseen observer.

"Oh, Joss, you're fucking me! You're fucking me! *Unggghhh!* Fuck me, fuck me harder for I will spend soon... keep fucking my cunt you great brute, you lovely lad... ohhh your beautiful cock is so big it's fair killing me!"

But Joss was unable to comply with her wishes. Kate saw him suddenly jump up to kneel and as he did so, extract his 'cock' that was all shiny and wet from its recent foray, give it a few squeezes with his fist and groan loudly as spurt after spurt of thick, milky-white liquid issued from its engorged tip (Kate had seen stallions urinating, but this was quite different, she thought). The thick, creamy liquid spattered Rosie's belly and even the underside of her big, pink-nippled breasts. Her hand flew to her sex, all angry, red and gaping from its recent ordeal and worked it with a speed and violence that again shook the virginal Kate to the core, for in no time Rosie was quivering and shuddering, all pink in the face and upper chest and wailing like a banshee.

For a few moments they lay together, limbs entwined, and then Rosie started to rub the sticky pools of Joss's mysterious white liquid into her breasts and over her belly, laughing softly, throatily. She coated her fingers in the slimy stuff and brought them to her mouth, sucking each dripping digit in turn with a look of intense lust on her face.

"Mmm... you taste good, Joss. I like to have your warm, creamy spunk in my mouth. I'll suck you off any time you like, but you know that, don't you just, you rascal!"

For the first time, Kate became aware of a smell, a warm, musky smell that was unlike any other of the human body's odours she was familiar with. Her nostrils flared and a prickle of excitement seemed to electrify her most sensitive body parts, a tingling and quivering quickened her senses. It seemed to her the most exotic, seductive and mysterious of perfumes, and from then on, whenever she encountered it again, she would always recognise it as the smell of sex and it would have the same aphrodisiac effect upon her as it did now. Only now she was still quite ignorant of why her body was responding in this way.

Kate sat quietly in her hiding place, her mind in uproar. So this was how men and women created their progeny! It was so... *bestial*, she thought. And yet, it had stirred some deep emotions within her and before she knew what she was doing, her hand stole between her thighs and felt her own, less mature sex. To her horror it was all wet! But surely – she had not lost control of her bladder, nor was it her time of month? What could it be? She brought her fingers to her mouth and tasted and smelled what was on her fingers... it was familiar and yet, different. It was slightly sweet and not unpleasant and once more she felt curiously grown-up. It was a rite of passage; the quintessential moment where childhood seemed to recede and adult life strongly beckon.

Tentatively she rubbed her own sex as she had seen Rosie doing. It was all slippery and felt almost indecently good. Now she looked at the thick tube of flesh that lay across Joss's thigh, no longer stiff, no longer threatening and thought she would like to take its pink head (which now seemed to have retreated under a thin covering of skin, although she was fascinated to see that she could still make out its contour) in her own mouth and caress it with her tongue, just as she had seen Rosie doing. Kate even felt an irrational jealousy of the older girl's experience. For the first time she became aware of a fleshy, wrinkled bag under Joss's softening sex that seemed to bulge with two spherical objects, and that, too, was fascinating to her. She rubbed her sex again, her middle finger now easily slipping into the slick groove between her excited, swelling labia. All sorts of wonderful, but unfamiliar sensations coursed through her body, centring in that critical spot where her thighs met her belly.

There was a noise in the distance and the couple had quickly left, dragging on their clothes and disappearing from her line of sight. A man and his dog came by, the reason for their swift departure.

Kate left her hiding place as soon as she was decently able to. Gathering up her long skirts, she ran all the way back to her house where, as usual, her father was reading and writing, deep in his books. But her heart lifted when she saw Mrs Proctor in the kitchen making bread, her sleeves rolled up and a floury apron protecting her dark dress.

Kate was bursting with things to say and ask, but did not know quite where to begin.

"Have you been birdsnesting again, young lady?"

Kate flushed pink and looked guilty.

"How did you know?"

Mrs Proctor looked up from her kneading, mildly surprised.

"I didn't, really – you often come back with a nest or an egg to show me. But you look upset, young Katie. Is everything alright?"

The note of gentle concern in Mrs Proctor's

voice triggered a violent reaction from Kate, who sat down on a kitchen chair and started to weep uncontrollably, her shoulders heaving with emotion. Between gradually diminishing sobs, she recounted all that she had just seen to the kindly housekeeper who placed a floury, maternal arm around her.

"Well now, child, I expect that they'll be getting married soon and that what you saw just showed how much they loved one another and just couldn't wait for their wedding day.

There live no birds, however bright or plain,
But rear a brood to take their place again.

They'll be rearing a brood together, soon enough, I'll wager."

Kate thought Mrs Proctor sounded rather unconvinced, however, and waited for her to continue.

"But there again maybe they were just enjoying being young," and here she sighed heavily, "because, Lord knows, I used to love playing their game when my Jack was alive."

She looked down comfortingly at Kate and gave her a reassuring hug.

"Your turn will come soon enough, Katie my pet. Why, in a year or two you'll be a fine young lady and ripe for marriage, to be sure. And when you find your husband you will have all those bodily and spiritual delights married life brings with it."

"And will my husband put his John Thomas, his cock, into my cunt? And will he fuck me like Joss fucked Rosie?"

Mrs Proctor winced slightly and coloured, and Kate was surprised to see that she looked mildly discomfited.

"Why yes, my darling, no doubt he will, but you must not say those words to any but your dearest, for they are words that only lovers use between one another. Now then, child, be off with you, for you have learned far more today than I could ever tell you of the matter." And she gave Kate another hug and gently pushed her out into the kitchen garden to gather some broad beans for supper. Over the next weeks and months, Kate learned all she needed to know from Mrs Proctor, even as to why the feelings of pleasure that she had experienced by her own hand came back to taunt her again and again when she was alone in bed at night. Kate never returned to the little bower in the hedgerow. But in her mind she would often revisit that place and secretly spy upon Joss and Rosie as they took their pleasure with one another, and her hands would feverishly seek out those places that would bring her a very similar pleasure until she drifted off to sleep, her dreams full of a dark, good-looking young suitors and their hard, penetrating cocks.

* * *

So when Mr Belfont had suggested that matrimony might be the best career for her, Kate had heartily agreed. It was indeed her desire to marry, and to marry well, too. She rather thought that a handsome young man, preferably wealthy and titled, would do rather well (although possibly good looks and wealth alone would be enough). It so happened that an old comrade from university, Sir Bradley Fordham, had written to Mr Belfont about an entirely different matter and had, by way of digression, mentioned that he and his wife Alice were seeking a governess for their daughter, Eleanor. Mr Belfont had written back post haste to suggest Miss Spencer for the position. Apparently the recommendation of an old varsity friend won the day, and the pretty young orphan was now on her way to a new life with, as Mr Belfont had put it, 'some thoroughly decent people'.

"How much further to Walthrop?" Kate asked.

The older coachman half turned in his seat to face his passenger and smiled indulgently at the note of impatience in her voice.

"Oh, only a couple of miles, Miss. Should be there in no time now."

The carriage drew up at the lodge gates of

Walthrop House. A cheerful, fat, gatekeeper's wife emerged from the lodge to swing the heavy gates back and allow them to continue the last stage of their journey up a long, gently curving drive, lined with dark green laurels and tall, graceful deciduous trees. Half apprehensive, half excited, Kate gave a little gasp of delight as they rounded the drive's last bend to see the elegant, golden façade of Walthrop House, a fine eighteenth century villa set in carefully tended parkland.

Moments later in the front hall the new governess was being greeted warmly by her future employers, Sir Bradley and Lady Fordham and their daughter, Eleanor. The coachmen, housekeeper and maids busied themselves with the new arrival's luggage.

* * *

After all the necessary introductions and arrangements had been made, Kate was taken on a tour of the house and gardens by Eleanor. She was a pretty, instantly likeable young girl, only too eager to make the best possible impression on her new governess. As the shadows lengthened on the immaculately kept lawns behind the house, Kate began to warm to the charming sixteen-year-old, who, although not the sharpest knife in the box, had as lively and affectionate a nature as anyone's she'd ever met.

Young Eleanor was petite. She had a typical 'English rose' fair complexion with an appealing face and sweet, sincere expression. Her nose was slightly *retroussé* and her hair was blonde and wavy, and grew almost down to her waist. Her bosom was not yet completely formed, but showed promise, Kate thought, and in any case, it complimented her girlish figure. As they entered a walled kitchen garden, in a gesture of unassuming friendliness, Eleanor took Kate's hand in her own, looked with great seriousness into her eyes and said, "Please, Miss Spencer, will you call me Ellie? It's my pet name, everyone I like calls me so."

Kate was touched by the young girl's implied offer of friendship and she smiled and gave Ellie's hand a little squeeze by way of saying 'yes'. The squeeze was immediately reciprocated and, impulsively, Ellie bent down and gave her startled governess's hand an ardent kiss.

"Oh, oh Miss Spencer, I'm sure that we shall be *such* good friends. I just *know* we will!"

Kate smiled and murmured her agreement.

"I'm sure we shall, Ellie. But you must be a good and diligent pupil, too, if you are to learn what your Papa and Mamma are so keen for me to teach you."

* * *

That evening, Kate came down to supper wearing her dress of grey silk with a small neat white collar; for a smarter effect she had supplemented this with a plain silk lilac shawl worn over her shoulders. Mary Belfont had advised her that, until she had found her bearings in her new home, she should proceed with caution, not appear too loud or clever, speak only when spoken to by her employers and address most of her conversation to her young charge, Eleanor. Even so, she was a little disappointed that her appearance seemed so drab compared to that of Eleanor and her mother who were both wearing the latest Worth fashions, beautifully made from finest silk and taffeta and shimmering in the soft, flickering light of the silver candelabra.

She sat on Sir Bradley's left and they discussed young Ellie's curriculum while mother and daughter chattered on to each other about the events of the day. Sir Bradley was a good-looking man for his age, which Kate put at about 45. He sported neatly trimmed side-whiskers and a luxuriant moustache and had a similar, fair complexion to that of his daughter. Kate was a little nervous of him at first, but he had a comfortable, charming manner that soon put her at her ease. At nine o'clock they rose and went upstairs to a large drawing room, an elegant room, hung with ancestral portraits and sporting paintings; a welcoming fire flickered in the grate. The butler brought a large tray of after dinner drinks in and set it down on a small table in front of Lady Fordham who reclined informally on a huge tiger skin rug by the fire, the extravagant folds of her dress heaped up behind her.

Sir Bradley excused himself and the three women continued to talk as they sipped tea, with Kate entertaining her two female companions by telling them some of the history of her respectable, but humble upbringing. It was her first chance to compare her companions properly. For mother and daughter they seemed very unalike: Lady Alice Fordham was a raven-haired woman in her mid-thirties, with a sensual, exotic appearance, strong dark eyebrows, a full, sensuous mouth and big, expressive eyes; she was slightly taller than her daughter but a little shorter than Kate. Her figure was almost voluptuous: it had a superb bust and a tiny waist that flared into womanly hips and a bottom as full as a ripe peach.

"My dear Miss Spencer, we must not keep you a moment longer," said Lady Fordham during a lull in the conversation. "You will have had a most exhausting day and you really should retire immediately. Breakfast will be between half-past eight and nine o'clock, but one of the housemaids will bring hot water for your toilette at a quarter to seven. Do let me know if there is anything else you need and I'll have one of the servants take it to your room."

* * *

That night Kate was woken by a violent storm. Cracks of ear-splitting thunder made it impossible to sleep, rain lashed the windowpanes and the air seemed thick and muggy. Just as she thought the tempest was dying down and she was drifting back into an uneasy slumber, she heard the door open. In the dim light saw a slight, familiar figure steal into her room. Ellie Fordham – like Kate herself – wore a long white nightgown buttoned up to her neck. Her lustrous blond hair fell over her shoulders in the manner of a shawl.

"Ellie! Why, whatever are you doing here?" asked Kate sleepily.

"Oh, Miss Spencer! I was so terrified... the storm!"

The girl's voice did indeed sound frightened and tearful; Kate rose up to a half-sitting position in her bed. Ellie threw herself into her arms and hugged her governess tightly.

"There, there," Kate soothed the young girl, "it's only a thunder storm, nothing to be scared of. Why, we're all safe and snug in doors, are we not?"

By way of response, Ellie merely shivered and hugged her more passionately. Kate absently stroked the girl's hair. She could smell the fresh, sweet scent of this young girl's body, so warm and comforting against her own. She could feel the two springy, apple-like globes of her breasts as they pressed into her ribcage and she fancied that she could even feel their firm, protuberant nipples as well. Little by little, Ellie shifted her body so that they were lying side by side in the narrow bed. Little by little, Kate felt herself drifting back to sleep, her lids grew heavy and her breathing regular.

Kate started to dream. She was back in the hedgerow, in her secret coign of vantage, and she could hear a voice calling her. It was Rosie Jebb. She was saying, "I know you're in there, Kate Spencer! Come out! Come out this moment!" Shamefully, Kate emerged from her hiding place, no longer a fifteen year old, but a twenty-three year old. To her surprise, she was naked. They both were.

"My, but that's a lovely bushy fanny you have there, young Katie, let's give it a feel, shall we?" said Rosie and boldly put her hand between Kate's legs. Kate blushed scarlet, not because of what Rosie was doing to her but because she loved the feeling so much, and because she could feel her own wetness squelching between her thighs as they clamped together on Rosie's questing fingers.

"No, Rosie, no! Please Rosie, please don't, *don't!*" For Rosie's fingers had won the day and now they were tormenting her in the most delicious way, having found a familiar source of pleasure that was located where her sex-lips joined to form a little hood over that impudent button that was her clitoris. And now Mrs Proctor happened by, smiling and nodding at Kate encouragingly. She too was naked, still a fine figure of a woman, but to Kate's horror, an enormous John Thomas sprouted from between her thighs...

Kate woke up.

In the dim light of her bedroom, she could see that the girl whose hands she could feel between her legs was not Rosie Jebb but Ellie Fordham.

Her sixteen year old pupil was quite naked.

Ellie had thrown aside the sheets and blankets and had somehow managed to raise Kate's nightdress, too. She had also unbuttoned the cotton garment so that Kate's full breasts now lay outside it, quite exposed and Ellie's hungry lips were causing the young governess deliciously erotic feelings as they licked and sucked her nipples with passion. But it was Ellie's fingers that were causing her the most pleasure as they busied themselves between the folds of her cunt.

For several critical moments, Kate was unable to speak. So confused was her waking mind, that for a time she was unable to distinguish between dream and reality. It was impossible to stop the blissful sensations that swept over her body, that thrilled her senses so. But a tiny corner of her consciousness told her that what was happening was very wrong indeed, that she must stop it, and right away, too.

"Oh Miss *Spencer!*" murmured her young ravisher disingenuously, "you are so *very* beautiful. Please forgive me but I simply could not help myself, lying next to you and feeling your lovely, soft, warm body next to mine."

Kate realised, with another shock, that the young girl's legs were intertwined with her own, and that Ellie was rubbing her sparsely-haired, wet little sex against her thigh with an increasing urgency. At the same time, her nimble fingers worked the governess's drenched labia and clitoris until the sensations that this caused became almost unbearable. Finally, Kate found her voice.

"*Ellie!* You must... *ohhh!* you must stop that at *once!* Please... what you do is not... it is very *wrong!*"

Her voice died away to a tortured gasp as Ellie somehow redoubled her efforts and managed to find a rich seam of the purest pleasure between her teacher's legs. Kate, half-frightened, half-ecstatic, became aware that she was rapidly loosing control of her body. She started to shudder and shake, to twitch and shiver as if gripped by a strong fever. Her mouth opened and, to her horror, she let out a loud and involuntary howl of delight...

Just then Ellie started to give a series of little screams as she, too, started to tremble with a near-orgasmic enjoyment.

Kate was about to make one last valiant attempt to prevent the explosion of physical pleasure that was welling up inside her when the door to her room was flung open and a shaft of light fell upon the bed. Lady Fordham stood there, holding an oil lamp aloft, and gazed down at the writhing tangle of naked legs and arms in front of her. She could see how her nude daughter's thighs continued to grip and relax, still in the dying throes of orgasm. She looked down upon Kate's semi-naked body as well and noted her proud breasts, the shine of juices that flowed at the junction of her legs and that the beatific expression on her face that was fast changing to one of guilty horror and dismay.

"*Eleanor!*"

A furious Lady Fordham literally spat out the name. There was no need to say any more. Little Ellie jumped up and, pulling on her nightgown, sidled past her mother and out of the door without so much as a backwards glance at Kate, who could just hear the soft patter of her retreating footsteps as the young girl escaped to her bedroom.

But Ellie was not to get off so lightly. Kate remained frozen as Alice Fordham wheeled around, set the lamp on the table by the door and strode rapidly after her daughter. There was the sound of a sharp slap, a terse admonitory lecture and loud sobs. A door slammed and, to her very great apprehension, Kate heard her employer's returning footsteps.

She quickly pulled her nightdress down, pulled on a pair of drawers, then jumped down from the bed and stood, buttoning herself up so that her breasts were once more covered. She could hardly bring herself to look Lady Fordham in the face when she once more stood in her bedroom. When she did, to her amazement, the older woman was smiling.

"That girl! Such a silly young thing, but she has a good heart…"

Alice Fordham advanced on Kate until she was only inches away from the confused governess. Her steady gaze held Kate riveted in place. "Well, my dear, your pretty little governess's body is really most beguiling. No wonder my daughter was so seduced," the taller woman mused. "Now that I've seen what's on offer, there's really no need to cover it all up again."

And as she said this, she began unbuttoning the top buttons of Kate's nightgown.

Kate was too flabbergasted to do more than gape. Then she made a feeble attempt to pull herself together and brush away the older woman's hands, but failed. "But-but, Lady Fordham, you're married... a mother...," Kate spluttered. "Surely you can't ..." She was unable to finish the sentence, the words failed her.

"Prefer my own sex? Be a sister of Sappho? A *Lesbian?*" Lady Fordham finished for her in tones of mock-horror as she pulled the nightdress down to reveal Kate's bosom. "No, not really, or rather, not strictly. My, those are pretty breasts," she sighed. "Those pretty, pink little nipples are so eager and alert."

Kate shivered. Lady Fordham was teasing her nipples, and they liked it! Their reaction astonished and dismayed Kate. She flapped her arms loosely.

"Pretty, pretty, pretty," Lady Fordham crooned softly, pinching Kate's delicate pink nipples, rolling them between her long, graceful fingers, tugging them outward to stretch Kate's beautifully shaped breasts provocatively. "I do not love women exclusively," Lady Fordham explained. "I enjoy the pleasures either sex can afford me."

"But your husband, Sir Bradley," Kate blurted out, trying desperately to fight the tremors of lust that were once more shaking her.

"My husband knows all about it," Lady Fordham answered easily. "As a matter of fact, he finds it rather enjoyable. Sometimes I bring my women friends home and we have some truly interesting variations."

Kate shook her head in futile denial. Her nightdress had been unbuttoned and she was naked to the waist. She wanted to break and run, but something held her rooted to the spot.

"Let's compare breasts, shall we?" Alice Fordham asked, undoing her own nightgown to let her large, lush breasts fall free. Then she ran her hands up, cupped them and ran her thumbs over the nipples.

"Aahhhh, that's so much better. We're both very fortunate – not needing any artificial support."

Kate's eyes were glued to the older woman's larger breasts. They were magnificent glands, full and round and heavy, with no sag. Her skin was very pale and the nipples were large sturdy buds, dimpled at the tips, and surrounded by large areolas. Kate had the insane urge to touch those heavy, warm masses, to measure their firmness and weight. She lifted her hands hesitantly.

"Yes, touch them," Alice Fordham purred. "Lift them and feel them. Feel how soft they are, and warm and heavy. Feel them."

Kate's mind was still reeling from the events of the past few minutes. She touched the handsome woman's full, lush breasts with gentle fingers and an electric thrill passed up her arms from her fingertips. Nothing in the world could feel so soft and warm and inviting. Kate wanted to bury her face in the deep, scented valley between them. She managed to restrain herself, and continued just cupping and lifting the two marvellously heavy, exciting globes. Then she ran her thumbs over the rubbery nipples, the way she loved to do with her own.

"Ahhhh," Lady Fordham sighed. Then she reached down to take the hem of Kate's nightdress and lifted it up over her hips. She started to feel under the bunched folds and Kate could feel her gentle, searching hands as they explored the contours of her hips and bottom. Her hand insinuated itself between Kate's drawers and the furry mound of her dripping sex and tickled her there, teasingly, lingeringly.

"Oh! I see that my daughter has prepared the way, so to speak."

Kate blushed furiously and fastened her attention completely on the breasts she was exploring with her hands. She was aware of her employer's hands becoming bolder. She was afraid she would go mad if she thought of anything other than the soft, graceful beauty of Alice Fordham's breasts. She thought neither of what was happening to her, nor of what was going to happen to her. All that mattered was the soft, warm and thrilling globes of flesh in her hands.

Kneeling briefly, Lady Fordham rolled Kate's drawers down her slim, strong legs and off. She planted a lingering kiss on her belly, just below Kate's navel, then dragged a wet tongue the short distance to her pubic bush. Kate felt Lady Fordham's saliva dry cool on her skin. Then, as she stood up, she once more stroked her hands the length of Kate's nude body, up the backs of her legs, over her buttocks, and up her back.

That simple, straightforward caress melted the remnant of resistance that was left in Kate. The enormous relief of Lady Fordham's apparent lack of concern at the compromising situation with Ellie that she had discovered when she had entered Kate's room – and her own passionate nature – had her seething with sexual need. She was a willing, eager toy in Lady Fordham's hands now.

Lady Fordham was ready to make full use of the shapely girl standing almost nude before her. This was the most exciting encounter she had had in a long time. The lithe, slim, healthy body of Kate Spencer was the most exciting she had ever seen. She held Kate's eyes now, and saw the surrender in them. Gently, but firmly, she drew Kate toward her, and licked her lips in anticipation.

Willingly, Kate tilted her head for the kiss she knew was coming, and closed her eyes submissively. Lady Fordham's lips were warm and moist and thrilling, working softly, easing Kate's lips open to admit a probing tongue. Warm soft breasts pressed against Kate's chest and then there was a warm, feminine body against hers. Kate could smell the exciting expensive scent that Alice Fordham was wearing. She had noticed it earlier that evening when they were in the drawing room. Kate touched her employer with her hands, slid them around her, then Kate was pressing the older woman as tightly against herself as Lady Fordham was pressing her.

The young governess was whirled away on a tidal wave of unexpected, lesbian pleasure.

The experience of being semi-nude in the arms of another woman who was also nearly naked, meanwhile indulging in a devouring sexual kiss, was unlike anything Kate had ever experienced: this major engagement made the brief encounter with Ellie seem a light skirmish by comparison. The skin against her own soft silky skin was just as soft and silken, with none of the harsh scratchiness of what she guessed a man's skin would be. The muscles embracing her were soft and feminine and tender, not hard and demanding as she imagined a man's would be. There were breasts against her breasts – soft yielding pillows instead of the hard pectoral muscles she had sometimes dreamed of so vividly.

Kate whimpered as she and Lady Fordham tumbled sideways onto the bed. She let Lady Fordham roll them over in a thrilling tangle of sleek, feminine limbs. With legs interlocked, Kate was pressing her warm, juicy cunt against Lady Fordham's smooth thigh, and felt Lady Fordham's thick, springy pubic hair scrubbing her own thigh.

Freeing one hand, Kate slid it between them, squeezed it between the resilient flesh of her breasts and Lady Fordham's to fondle the other woman's spongy mammary glands. At the same time, Kate slid her other hand down the sleek, smooth graceful curve of the older woman's back and cupped one of the woman's lush, yielding buttocks, then hauled her employer's pelvis tight against her own.

The two women formed an erotic tangle of smooth, female bodies on the small four-poster. Kate's slender, slimmer frame pressed and twined tightly with her employer's fuller and more womanly body.

Alice Fordham broke the kiss at last, flicking her tongue out to lap at Kate's cheek, the side of her throat, her delicate, sensitive ear. With a soft, excited sigh, Kate rolled onto her back, maintaining contact with her bedfellow with one hand, brushing her heavy, swaying breasts, first one and then the other.

Her seducer licked daintily at the side of Kate's throat, and Kate turned her head to give the older woman better access to her. Kate's face was a mask of pure lust as she submitted to the other woman's caresses.

Tongue working delicately, Alice Fordham eased her way downward, lapping now on Kate's upper chest, tracing long wet strokes with her tongue. The clean, innocent scent of soap still clung to Kate's skin, inflaming the older woman's desire even further. The delicate, shy touch of Kate's inexperienced fingers on her breasts sent delicious, electrical jolts through Lady Fordham.

Brushing a lock of her own hair aside, Lady Fordham touched her tongue to one of

Kate's nipples, flicking her rubbery nubbin excitingly.

Kate sucked in her breath as the jolt of that oral caress blazed through her. Her hand cupped and lifted one of the other woman's full breasts, feeling the hard nipple press into her hand. Kate's hips were beginning to roll and twist impatiently.

Her soft black hair brushing Kate's heaving chest, Lady Fordham shifted her mouth to Kate's other breast, sucking on the turgid, begging nipple, scraping it with her tongue. Then she pulled away and looked down on Kate tenderly.

"Please," Kate pleaded softly, looking into Lady Fordham's face longingly. "Please, don't stop."

"Open your legs wide, girl – show me your pretty little sex."

Kate did as she was told, lying back on the bed and spreading her thighs wide. With one hand she pulled back the hood of her clitoris so that the inflamed pink pearl of flesh was revealed to Alice Fordham who lost no time in starting to lick and suck it, then letting a stiff, enquiring tongue wander all over her young *protégée's* engorged labia.

"Mmmm... so juicy, so sweet... just like a bunch of warm, crushed grapes!"

Lady Fordham looked up briefly and Kate could see in the golden light of the oil lamp

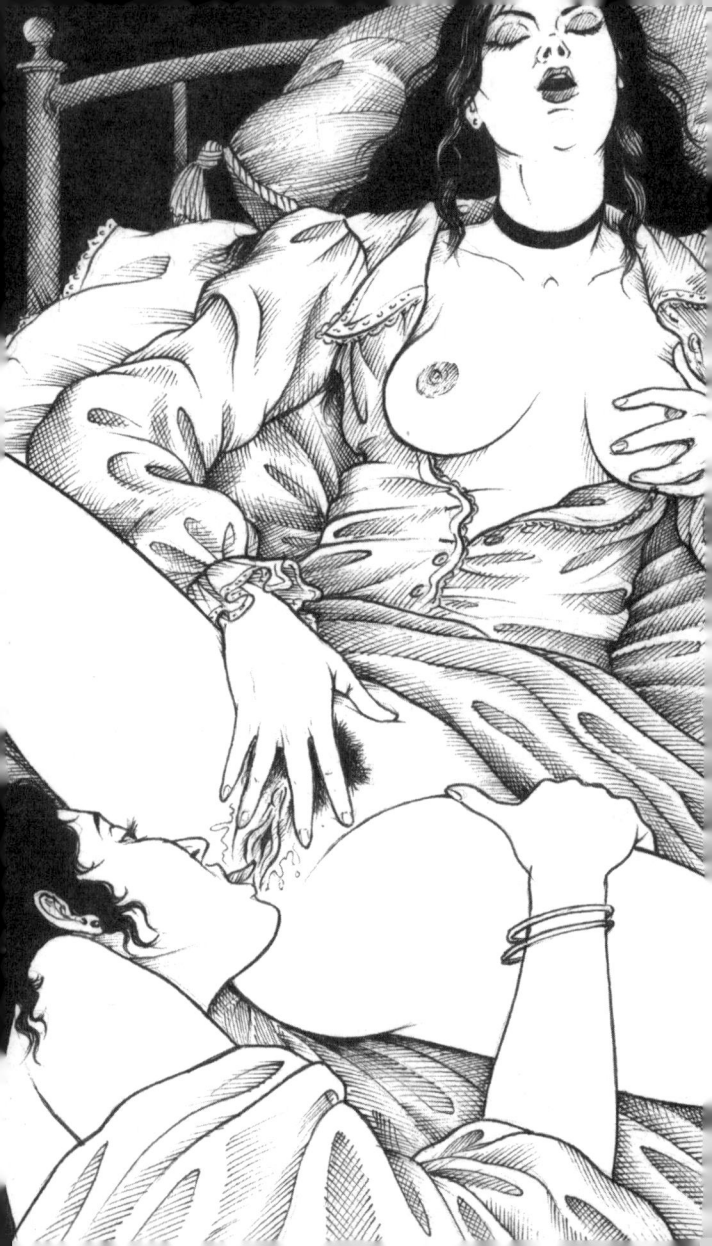

that her mouth and chin were shiny with juice. She could smell her lust – and that of her companion, and far from being repelled by such a vulgar bodily odour, she revelled in its musky, sweet earthiness. Lady Fordham's tongue was as slippery as an eel, delving far into Kate's vagina, sliding into every fleshy crevice, even titillating her sensitive anus.

The girl closed her eyes and revelled in the voluptuous sensations. This was very different to what she had experienced with Ellie, whose fumblings now seemed almost childish by comparison. Alice Fordham was playing her as a fisherman plays a fish, varying the intensity of her attack; at times she could only feel the merest glide of her tongue, the merest brush of her full lips. Then she would feel the full power of the older woman's lesbian skills, a tongue that stabbed repeatedly, fingers that tickled and delved, lips that sucked her labia and blew a stream of warm breath over her clitoral bud. And from far away, Kate felt that a sensation more wonderful than she had ever experienced was imminent.

For her part, though she was nearly overcome by her own mounting lust, Alice Fordham was surreptitiously feeling for Kate's maidenhead under the guise of stimulating her with her fingers.

She smiled exultantly: she could feel the girl's hymen!

When suddenly it all ceased, Kate almost cried out aloud. She was brought down to earth from her clouds of rising passion with a bump. She raised herself on her elbows and watched as Lady Fordham pushed down her own nightgown to reveal a pale, luscious body. Her bush was black: thick, curling, and mysterious, nestled between strong, graceful, alabaster thighs.

"You'll do to me what I do to you?" Lady Fordham asked softly, not wanting a passive partner in their coupling.

"Yes," Kate choked out. "Yes, anything, only please, *please*, don't stop now."

Lady Fordham turned and her head swept down toward Kate's crotch. Kate let her thighs fall open again, hungry for the probing she knew would return, and committing herself to placing her mouth upon the other woman's dripping labia.

Lady Fordham lifted one leg over Kate's head as she once again pressed her face into the soft, brown bush between Kate's trim, sleek thighs. She was smothered in the exciting smell of the girl's aroused cunt. She pressed her tongue into the metallic-salty flesh between the labia, probing deep into the honey'd hole of Kate's dripping vagina. While Lady Fordham chewed ecstatically on Kate's dripping folds of flesh she lowered her own crotch onto Kate's face.

Kate was blazing with lust, wave after fiery wave of overpowering sexual pleasure. Her hips were jerking and twisting as she thrilled to having her fanny devoured. She almost laughed aloud at the extraordinary pleasure of her first sexual experience. No... her *second*, she smiled to herself. She saw Lady Fordham's thickly-bushed crotch descending on her face, and closed her eyes and wetted her lips nervously. Now, in the lamp's soft light, she could observe at impossibly close quarters the split of the woman's hairy outer labia and the oozing, swollen red inner lips that formed the impressive, fleshy curtains to her vaginal passage. A single drop of syrupy female juice dripped down onto her nose and trickled slowly down onto her upper lip. Just before Alice Fordham's cunt descended further, Kate caught sight of her puckered brown anus, and saw that, unlike her own, this opening was quite darkly pigmented and hirsute, surrounded by a wreath of curling black hairs.

Then her nose was pressing into thick wiry curls and her mouth on the soft, juice-slick lips of Lady Fordham's cunt; she was smothered in the thick musky scent of the older woman's feminine secretions. Hesitantly at first, then with a driving, vulgar need, Kate drilled her tongue into Lady Fordham's oozing, dripping sex, probing as deeply as she could into her slimy vagina, working her jaw against the pulpy folds of flesh. Lady Fordham's hips began to twist and heave, mashing Kate's head back into the pillows. Kate fought back by trying to bore more deeply into the smothering cunt engulfing her face. Her mouth filled with fluid and she had to swallow repeatedly. As she increased Lady Fordham's searing lust, Kate was rewarded by increased efforts on the part of her employer. The voluptuous woman's mouth was sliding, seeking. Suddenly lips closed around Kate's clitoris, and Kate's whole body exploded into glittering fragments. The moment had arrived and she twitched and moaned spastically as Alice Fordham mercilessly continued to suck and finger her cunt.

"Spend, young Kate, that's right, *spend!*"

Half out of her mind from her very first real orgasm, Kate instinctively sought the large, fleshy bean of Lady Fordham's clitoris with her own lips. She sucked juicy, quivering, oozing folds of flesh between her lips, found the pearl of Lady Fordham's nerve-laden button, and lashed it wildly with her tongue.

Lady Fordham's hips suddenly cut loose in a titanic heave and Kate lost her target. Frantically, Kate wrapped her arms around Lady Fordham's hips and clutched at her large and beautiful bottom to restrain her convulsive heaving and keep contact with her clitoris. At the same time, Kate's own hips were heaving, slamming her pubis into Lady Fordham's working, sucking, stimulating, hungry mouth.

The Sapphic coupling degenerated into a quivering, twitching tangle as the two orgasms went on and on and on. Faces were mashed against crotches, squeezed between clutching thighs. Juicy, wet, slurping eating sounds filled the room for a long time. Eventually, sexual and muscular exhaustion released the women from their torment. Then they simply lay limp, Lady Fordham still on top of Kate.

Finally, she rolled off. Gloriously, shamelessly nude, Lady Fordham went to the washstand and poured a little water onto a dry flannel. She returned with the damp cloth. Sitting on the side of the bed, she tenderly washed the saliva and vaginal oozings from Kate's face. Then she carefully bathed the young governess's battered sex and the insides of her thighs.

Kate didn't move. Mentally, emotionally, and physically, her mind reeled from the uninhibited lesbian experience. She felt tempted to burst into tears.

"Kate Spencer, you are a young tigress, who would have guessed there beat a passionate heart within that apparently chaste breast?" Lady Fordham commented, breaking the silence at last.

Kate stared at the woman miserably.

"Why so sad?" Lady Fordham said, comfortingly. "Will you seek a young man, a consort, with any less enthusiasm now?"

"No-o," Kate acknowledged hesitantly after a moment's thought.

"Exactly. Men and women just have different things to offer. I like cock just as much as I like cunt, and I'll suck cock as eagerly as I'll eat cunt."

Kate was shocked. The forbidden words seemed to trip so easily off the woman's aristocratic lips. From her well-spoken mouth the words sounded doubly obscene. Kate shook her head, still utterly bewildered. "Lady Fordham... Has the world gone mad? I... I don't really understand what has happened to me."

"Neither would I were I in your shoes, you sweet girl, it's always like that the very first time," Lady Fordham reassured her. "But no, the world has not gone mad, although in matters of love sometimes it will seem very topsy-turvy – just like *Alice in Wonderland!* Which reminds me," and the beautiful, dark-haired woman gave a conspiratorial little laugh, "when we are alone together, you must always call me Alice. Now will you give me a kiss before I go?"

Kate put her heart and her soul into the

kiss she gave the older woman. Their lips parted, their tongues intertwined, danced and duelled. They met, woman to girl, mistress to employee, but still equals in this long, honest embrace.

Chapter Two

Alice Fordham woke the next morning in the best of moods. But it did not last long. The housekeeper, Mrs Beveridge, knocked on her bedroom door and was now interrupting her ladyship's breakfast to tell her that Miss Spencer, the new governess, had packed her bags, if you please, and was waiting in the morning room for Lady Fordham and Sir Bradley to come down, as she wanted to give her notice.

Her mistress steepled her fingers under her chin and thought.

"Stupid girl," she said finally, to no one in particular. "Get me my writing case, will you please, Mary?"

Mrs Beveridge, a hatchet-faced woman in her early fifties, gave a superior little smile and brought the shagreen and rosewood case over to her mistress's bed. Alice wrote rapidly in pencil on a sheet of notepaper, folded it twice and handed it to the housekeeper.

"Give that to Jenks. He'll know what to do. And Mary…"

"Yes, M'lady?"

"No one must know of this."

"Very good, M'lady."

Of course, once outside her mistress's room, Mary Beveridge read the note that Lady Fordham had written. After all, if she had not sealed it, it was fair game, she reasoned to herself. The housekeeper's eyebrows rose a little and she tut-tutted quietly to herself. Wearing a thin little smile, she placed the note in her *reticule* and hurried off to find the butler.

* * *

Alice, pale, tearful and trembling slightly, knew that she was doing the right thing. How could she possibly continue in the position of a governess if she had had carnal knowledge of both her employer and her pupil? The only choice open to her was that of handing in her notice. Surely Alice… Lady Fordham… would persuade her husband to give her a good reference? After all that had happened she had to understand.

As Alice and her husband entered the room, a pale and wan Kate rose shakily to her feet. They appeared more concerned than angry, she thought, slightly relieved. She hoped that the interview would be brief. She would stay in a hotel in Windsor until she could ascertain whether the kind, neighbourly Belfonts would have her back until she could find another post. She felt sure that they would...

"Oh Kate, I'm so sorry that you feel you cannot stay with us."

Alice Fordham contrived to look aggrieved, concerned and sad at the same time. Her husband leant his arm on the mantelpiece and, one foot on fender, fixed her with a sympathetic look and tugged at his moustache.

"Dashed shame, Miss Spencer. Hoped you might stay with us a bit longer, what?"

There was a pregnant pause while they waited for Kate to respond. She could think of nothing appropriate to say. Merely by glancing at Alice, her head immediately filled with images of the last night's unnatural lesbian couplings she had enjoyed with her and her daughter. Sir Bradley smiled at her encouragingly as if urging her to speak, perhaps to reconsider. What a kindly man! A new pang of guilt shot through her very core. And this was how she chose to repay his kindness – by such filthy, lewd, disgusting behaviour – the behaviour of a common street prostitute.

Just as she was about to deliver her

agonised and passionately sincere response, Jenks came in with only the most peremptory of knocks, went straight up to his Mistress and whispered urgently in her ear.

"I see. Kate, Jenks tells me that a valuable family treasure has gone missing – the Fordham Miniature. It was seen in its usual place, my husband's study, first thing in the morning. Now it is no longer there. None have entered or left the house. I hope you will not take this amiss, but we must search your luggage before you depart – if depart you really must."

"Of... of course, Lady Fordham. I would not object in the least," Kate said, rather primly.

Kate was dismayed. The Fordham Miniature was the most valuable of this noble old family's heirlooms. Painted by Nicholas Hilliard in Elizabethan times, it was worth a small fortune. And now she was suspected of being a thief? Perhaps she deserved no better, for if she had acted as if she were a wanton whore, why should they not assume she had the morals of a thief, also?

The small group moved from the morning room to the hall where Kate's luggage had been placed in a neat pile by the front door. Mrs Beveridge was already on her knees undoing the straps of Kate's trunk, while Lady Fordham went through one of the valises she had placed on the hall table. Kate saw her stiffen and she heard her slowly say in an icy voice and without turning around, "Jenks, Mary, you may leave us now. There is no need to search any further."

The servants left hurriedly, and when she heard the door close at the end of the hall, Alice turned to face her husband and Kate.

"Oh Kate. How *could* you?"

Kate gasped. Alice held the miniature in her hand.

"No... I mean... that is *impossible*... someone must have..."

Kate blushed. She blushed easily and now she blushed beetroot red, as if she were trying her very hardest to convince the Fordhams of her guilt.

Sir Bradley's handsome features, on the other hand, were livid. His lips narrowed in a thin line of anger and his jaw clenched in a most alarming manner. His fists clenched and unclenched spasmodically, and for a moment she thought that he might hit her.

"In my father's day, you would have been hung for far less a crime. I'm in half a mind to call the constable. I daresay you'd get a few years for this, my pretty miss!"

He turned on his heel and entered his study, slamming the door behind him.

Kate looked at Alice Fordham entreatingly, but the look on the beautiful face of her first lover was hard to gauge. The room seemed to start spinning around her and now she saw Alice Fordham's inscrutable look change to one of concern as Kate's vision clouded and darkened. She sank to her knees then fell on her side in a deep faint.

When she came to, she was lying on a *chaise longue* in the morning room. Sir Bradley was nowhere to be seen but Alice Fordham was mopping her brow with a dainty embroidered handkerchief dipped in cologne. Kate looked terrified, trapped in a nightmare that was all too real. She rose up, but Alice pushed her gently back and smiled reassuringly.

"It's alright, Kate. I know you didn't steal the miniature. But I have no idea how it ended up in your valise."

Oh thank God, thought Kate. Someone believes me. She closed her eyes and let out a little sigh of relief.

"But although I think I have mostly persuaded him, my husband is not yet as sure as I am. Yet. I shall, before too long, get to the bottom of this mystery. But there must be no more talk of leaving, for that would only convince my husband of your guilt. Now you must go to your room and rest. I will have some luncheon sent up for you, and I have told Ellie that you are feeling below the weather and that she is excused lessons for today."

"Oh thank you, thank you, thank you Lady Ford… Alice, thank you from the bottom of my heart…"

"You poor girl, Sir Bradley, you and I will dine *à trois* tonight. Ellie will have an early supper. I feel sure that we shall all be looking upon this morning's events as a storm in a teacup by then. However there are one or two things I would like you to do for me before you go up to your room."

At that moment Kate would have attempted to swim the Channel naked for Alice, had she asked her to.

"Certainly, Alice, what would you have me do?"

"Here is a contract of employment. It is really a document of no consequence, however it helps me to keep my affairs in order."

Kate signed the document in her neat hand.

"And this…" Alice gave a small deprecatory laugh, handing her another sheet, "…oh this is just one of Bradley's pet schemes… a sort of society that looks after fallen women, well… girls really. It's called the 'The Lord's Handmaidens'; it's run by a kindly local pastor, the Reverend Pike, who devotes his time to ameliorating the lot of these miserable girls, training them to take their place in society and even finding new positions for them when they leave. Its supporters, mainly local ladies from the parish's gentry, are called the 'Followers'. I would very much appreciate it if you became a 'Follower'."

Kate signed the second piece of paper and handed both documents back to Alice. She felt sure that this would help to give her a fresh start with the Fordhams.

And with this, Alice bent forward and gave Kate a chaste little kiss on her forehead.

* * *

That evening at dinner, her employers acted as if nothing had ever happened, but Kate felt that she was still on probation as far as Sir Bradley was concerned. He was charming as ever, but perhaps a little cooler towards her than the evening before. He told her a little about the home for destitute girls he ran on the estate with the help of a kindly pastor, the Reverend Pike.

The food was spicy and, being thirsty, Kate drank more wine than she was used to. Especially a very sweet *sauterne* that Sir Bradley insisted that she try with her desert. By the time they got up to go into the drawing room, she realised that she was somewhat unsteady on her feet. Sir Bradley offered her his arm, which she gratefully took.

Once more the fire had been lit, and Kate thought this strange, as tonight it was not particularly chilly. Once more, Lady Fordham sat and dispensed drinks from the tray that Jenks had set down before her. This time, her husband remained.

"That will be all, Jenks, you and the others may retire now."

When the butler had left the room, Alice bade Kate come and sit beside her on the floor.

"We shall be cosier thus, shan't we? And now the pasha can survey his harem of two."

They all laughed and any tenseness that Kate might have felt before evaporated completely. Alice pulled her gently down so that her head lay in the older woman's lap. She stroked Kate's hair and forehead, soothing her. It was all done in such a natural, almost sisterly, way that Kate thought little of it. Her mistress took a sip of cognac from the glass she was holding and bent down to kiss Kate's lips. She dribbled a little of the spirit inside her mouth. By now Kate was in such a warm, comfortable state that she felt this to be quite proper. Her limbs felt heavy, and she giggled foolishly as she took another mouthful of cognac from Alice's voluptuous lips.

She looked up and her eyes met Sir Bradley's. He was smiling indulgently, as if watching children play. He really was a fine figure of a man, thought Kate to herself and her eyes wondered to the area of his groin, where to her surprise and amusement she could see the outline of his John Thomas. It was enormous. What had Alice said to her? "Sometimes I bring my women friends home and we have some truly interesting variations..." In the soft glow of the candelabra and lamps she thought her employers had never looked so attractive.

So close to the fire, Kate felt hot. And when Alice started to remove her clothes, she found it was not only a relief, but a reassuring sign that she had been accepted back into the bosom of the Fordham family.

The voices of the others became distant, almost fading away entirely, returning occasionally loud and fragmented. Alice had freed her large breasts from the confines of her dress and the mere sight of them aroused feelings of lust. Kate's cunt started to lubricate.

"Look, dearest, see how wet her sex becomes!"

As Alice's fingers busily parted the folds of her sex, and rubbed either side of her clitoris, Kate dimly realised through the warm haze of lassitude that she was going to be fucked. She sincerely hoped so. Then she would become the second Lady Fordham. Part of the Fordham harem. She giggled inanely.

"Lick her cunt, Bradley. She tastes divine. Here let me hold her legs open for you... But not for too long. The poor little thing so desperately needs to be fucked! Yes, Kate," laughed her employer humiliatingly, "sweet little Kate, now you will be deflowered... for our pleasure!"

Kate felt a firm grip on her ankles as Alice Fordham lifted them up and over her head. For the very first time in her life, Kate Spencer's sex was entirely exposed to a man's gaze: he could see her dark brown pubic bush, the delicate, seeping, pink folds of her exquisite, virginal cunt – even the tight, wrinkled little pucker of her nut-brown anus.

Bradley Fordham needed none of his wife's encouragement. He quickly knelt and his fingers started to explore Kate's wet, pulsing sex.

She groaned and writhed deliriously beneath this determined attack on her genitals. She felt his fingers rubbing, sliding at the tender lips of her vagina, and slowly spreading them apart between her widely spread legs. Then a sudden pain as his middle finger probed her hymen too hard. In a sudden rush of irrational, girlish terror, she tried to clamp her thighs together but he was too quick, and besides, his wife was keeping a firm grip on her widespread ankles. His head dropped and the sudden wetness of his slavering lips locking onto her throbbing and exposed clitoris froze her body as it was. She felt the brush of his moustache, the tickle of his side-whiskers. A sharp new sensation rippled through her and she felt all the tingling carnal passions that she had built up over all the years before suddenly and without warning, rushing up from her legs and belly and gurgling from her mouth in an uncontrollable torrent of pleading cries.

"Lord! Oh Lord!" she groaned over and over without ceasing as the firm bud of her clitoris sprang into a life that she never knew it possessed as he nibbled and sucked mercilessly at it in the sudden crazed passion that now overtook him. Her head rolled from side to side on a strategically placed pillow, her hair coming loose from the carefully tied *chignon*, but it didn't matter. Nothing mattered now but the delicious rape of Bradley Fordham's mouth that was making those wet, sucking sounds down between her open and defenceless legs. Strange, muted and hazy thoughts of that summer day long ago with Rosie and Joss drifted across her mind and she wanted to open her eyes and see if there were lazy fleecy clouds above, but she couldn't – only the pale, looming orbs of Alice's breasts as they hung down, swaying slightly with the exertion of holding Kate's legs open. There was nothing she could do but buck and churn beneath that probing tongue that was burning fire into her young and unplundered vagina.

And then, when she thought it would never end, he twisted around again, dropping heavily between her legs. He paused to unbutton his trousers and allow his enormous cock to spring free.

Kate was beside herself, she had never felt so open and ready in her life. Her pelvis rotated in small hungry circles as he knelt between her open thighs, holding her legs in the air. He smiled down at her.

"You're a pretty, sporting, young girl, Miss Spencer. I think you will enjoy this as much as I will," said Sir Bradley in a voice tight with lust.

"Oh, Sir Bradley!" she gasped urgently, her pelvis making larger circles now. "Please put your cock in my cunt. Fuck me! Fuck me now or I shall surely die!"

The master of Walthrop gave a surprised little laugh at his innocent young governess's sudden descent into gutter-language. Without hesitation he pulled her under him, the softness of her buttocks sliding along the roughness of the carpet, and fell heavily down between her legs. His hand directed his huge throbbing cock to the wet, quivering lips of her cunt, pausing briefly to part the thick, chestnut pubic hair; gently he manoeuvred the glans until it slid down her labial groove and came to rest at the little mouth of her cringing vagina. Kate could feel Alice's hands squeezing her breasts, lightly pinching her nipples so that they became extremely stiff and erect. The sensation of this double stimulation was extraordinary and she wallowed in the luxury of its blissful effect.

Then she felt him push forward until his glans rested against the thin veil of virgin's flesh... her hymen, her maidenhead. There was a tightness of the sort that she herself had caused when exploring that mysterious part of her anatomy. But even in a condition of arousal or erotic excitement, even when she had been dripping wet, she had never even come close to the delicious feelings of utter surrender and submission that she was now experiencing. Sir Bradley was about to cull her virginity! The moment had arrived: she was on the threshold of womanhood!

The baronet looked up and caught the eye of his wife, and saw that her tongue was caressing the underside of her upper lip, something that she did only when acutely aroused. His cockhead was maddeningly, unsatisfyingly contained by the very light grasp of Kate's labial folds. He needed to feel the tightness of this prim young governess's cunt. He needed to, no, he *had* to fuck her.

With this irresistible imperative, Bradley thrust his hips forward, his impossibly large and stiff cock ripping the tender flesh of her hymen irreparably and bursting into the wonderfully enveloping tightness of her vaginal passage. At the same time, Alice squeezed both Kate's nipples as hard as she could, knowing that the two distinctive pains would help to cancel each other out.

"Aaaagggghhhbh!" Kate screamed, the hot, blinding pain seared deep in her belly. "Oooooh, God – *stop!* Sir, you are killing me. Oh... please... *please*...!" Her eyes flew open and she looked, panic-stricken, from one lust-warped face to the other.

Her arms jerked up involuntarily and she clung to Bradley with all her strength as though it might drive the pain away. Her face was contorted and eyes screwed tightly shut. She struggled once, but then her body stilled to ease the pain. She could feel the full length of the huge penis throbbing deep inside her vagina, imbedded to the hilt. Tiny whimpers escaped her tightly closed lips as she lay quietly, adjusting to the new and strange invasion of her tight virginal cunt.

Sir Bradley did not move at first, but lay rigid on top of her. He had half-doubted his wife's testimony of her virginity from the fervour with which she had entered into the act, but now he was reassured. She was a virgin all right and he knew it would take her a moment for the pain to subside. Then, then by God he would throw it to her as though she'd never get it again. He hadn't had a virgin for many months, and he wasn't going to let this one off easy.

In a moment, Kate made her first tentative movement. She rolled her buttocks slightly under him and a small surprised gasp of pleasure escaped from between her teeth.

It no longer hurt!

She had thought the pain would last much longer and she had been afraid of it, but suddenly there was none, a slight discomfort, yes, but coupled with the strange sensations coursing through her body it all merged into one great mass of indescribable pleasure.

Sir Bradley flexed his cock inside her.

"Oooooooh, yessss, do it," she whimpered softly up into his ear.

He did it again.

"Oh God, yessss! yessss!" she hissed, her hips suddenly and slowly beginning to rotate beneath him. The tight, wet walls of her cunt contracted possessively around the hardness of his cock as though it were frightened of losing it. He groaned as he felt the muscles deep inside her belly answering the pulsating throbs of his steel-hard shaft. He could hold himself back no longer and began a slow teasing grinding in and out between her wide spread thighs. He could feel the tightness of her clasping around him like soft warm India rubber, the walls of her cunt holding to him with an almost animal desperation as he withdrew slowly and then thrust forward again to sink his massive cock deep back down inside the young governess.

Her pelvis beneath him began a faster rotation now, her buttocks grinding and writhing down into the hardness of the ground with a sudden abandon that took him by surprise. Mewling sounds of passion and lust escaped her lips in waves of sound that he could not understand but that his body reacted to in the instinctive rhythm of intercourse that was as old as the hills. He levered up on his toes and dropped his hands down under them to cup the full quavering mounds of her buttocks so that he could fuck deeper down into her.

"Aaahhhhhg! Ooooooooh!" She groaned and twisted her body like a wild animal under him. Thrusting her loins up at him as he ground down into her to take the whole of his expanding cook far down inside the warm hot sheath of her vagina.

Kate rocked in a dream world of obscene and uncontrolled lust under his pounding body. She had never in all her life, not even with Alice, felt the way she did now with his huge male hardness buried to the hilt inside her. She could feel the soft slap of his balls against the tightly clenched cheeks of her buttocks and the strength of his hands as they kneaded and tore at her tender flesh as a baker's hands roughly knead dough. She struggled to open her thighs wider, to take him deeper, but she could not. He was sunk as far into her as he could go but she wanted more.

"Fuck harder... oh, Sir Bradley, please fuck me harder," she gasped as she felt him begin to thrust his massive hardness into her, now with longer and longer strokes. A strange dancing delight of fire was building far down in her quivering belly that drove her churning body on and on in it's wild quest for the delicious sensation building and building in every pore of her sweating body.

And then it came!

Her muscles contracted tightly around his plunging cock and she cried out wildly thinking the end was here, but soon his strong rhythmic strokes set off another explosion of delight that she had never dreamed possible. Her buttocks rotated against the carpet like a helpless ship caught in the vicious waves of a driving storm. She arched her back taught, her head buffeting against the ground, her hair fanning out, her full quivering breasts pointing to the sky, trembling and swirling in jerking

circles as she quickened her movements to meet the mounting urgency she could feel pulsating through the head of his throbbing rod sunk so deep inside her hungry vagina.

It was gentle at first, preceded by a soft, inhuman gurgle from deep within his chest. And then he let out a might roar as he withdrew and held his quivering cock over her defenceless, vulnerable torso. Hot white jets of his sperm erupted, splashing the skin of her belly and breasts with a warmth and sensation beyond all description. She could not resist snaking a hand between her legs and coaxing her battered sex, jerking her own legs uncontrollably out in the air on either side of his as a great flash of erotic fire leaped up inside her and exploded in the volcanic eruption of another orgasm for, after all, this was the fulfilment of such great expectations, and the memories of Joss and Rosie came flooding back; finally all was resolved – she knew now what the butcher's daughter had experienced that day in the fields, the last piece of the puzzle fell into place and now it all made perfect sense to her.

"Ahhh! Ahhh!" She moaned, her head turning from side to side, her hair beating the ground like a soft whip. The muscles of her hips and belly contracted in rolling waves of spasm, the pulsating walls of her hot, juice-filled fanny sucking at her delving fingers, until finally, weak and exhausted, she stopped and fell back limply.

They lay for some time, panting and gasping in the smell of her wet orgasm and the odour of the perspiration which coated their bodies in a light dewy film, while above them, the almost-forgotten Alice Fordham's fingers strummed and flicked a wet, hungry sex in a desperate quest for her own releasing climax while the fingers of her other hand squeezed and pinched the inflamed, swollen nipples of her lewdly exposed breasts.

"Oh, oh yes, my dears... I am spending... I am spending...oh... *now!*" she shrieked ecstatically.

Chapter Three

The next morning, Kate awoke with a splitting headache. As it was Saturday, she reasoned, there would be no lessons for Ellie, at least. She tried to review the events of the preceding evening but could only remember the main incidents with any clarity. Her disgraceful, drunken state... Sir Bradley deflowering her... taking her maidenhead... Alice looking on as if she approved of the whole shocking thing. She felt between her legs, where she was still sore. At least she was a woman now, she thought, ruefully. But this whole family seemed to be obsessed by... carnal knowledge! Sexual intercourse seemed to be their staple diet! Or had it been her fault again? Had she been too forward with Sir Bradley? Encouraged him? She was so unsure. Again, she thought of flight – of packing her things and leaving. But it was not as simple as it had been yesterday. Firstly, there was the contract she had signed – it lasted for a year. Then there was the whole sorry incident of the stolen miniature, even though she knew herself to be innocent, her innocence would be impossible to prove. And then there was the physical problem of her departure – she could hardly walk to Windsor as it was a very considerable distance on foot.

Kate smiled bravely to herself. She must make the very best of it. From now on she would simply avoid situations that might lead to... *that* sort of thing again.

Breakfast in the Fordham household was the least formal meal, for though Sir Bradley was to be found at the head of the dining room table, immersed in his newspaper with a young footman in attendance, Alice and Ellie put in no more than token appearances. Kate was grateful, in many ways, that Sir Bradley gave her no more than a curt nod when she appeared to take her place; when she enquired about the possibility of a church service, he became more animated.

"There are two possibilities," he told her, "but only one that I would recommend to you: that of the Reverend Pike – his place of worship is but a stone's throw from this house."

Sir Bradley seemed disinclined to continue the conversation much further and Kate held her council accordingly. Later she found his wife in the kitchen garden gathering sweet peas in a flower basket.

"Aren't they pretty, Kate? I always think that they are the most *feminine* of flowers..."

"Lady Fordham... Alice... I... I am so very sorry for what happened last..."

"Did you enjoy yourself?"

"Yes, very much, but..."

But Kate was cut short as Alice Fordham replied brusquely, "Nonsense, my dear girl. No 'buts', if you enjoyed it, then there's no need for anyone to apologise. Think of it merely as a new and salutary experience."

Kate smiled her brave smile, but inwardly she thought that it was all very well for Alice to make so little of the lewd behaviour of the previous night that had led so inexorably to her defloration, but she surely realised that this was a momentous event in her, Kate's, life. Her emotions were running feverishly high and she was in great need of a sisterly shoulder to lean, if not cry, upon.

Alice must have felt some of Kate's inner turmoil, since she spoke in a softer, more solicitous tone when she said, "Dearest Kate, when we attend the Hall of Worship this evening, you will no doubt have an audience with the good Reverend. He is a little eccentric, perhaps, but a visionary in his own, peculiar way. And then there is his special little welcoming ceremony – all new members of our small sect enjoy it immensely. Quite apart from the spiritual comfort that I sense you to be in need of, I am quite sure that you will see things more in proportion after your initiation. And you will also find life here at Walthrop far, far more agreeable once you feel yourself to be more a part of our local community."

Kate received Alice's little speech with mixed feelings. In part she was even more troubled that such a momentous rite of passage for her could be made so light of, in part she was mightily relieved that once more, such a major moral transgression seemed to have been commuted to a minor incident, a 'salutory experience' no less. Perhaps she was out of touch after years of rural exile. Perhaps it was time to adjust her simple moral code so that it was more in tune with that of these patently more sophisticated folk.

The rest of the morning passed uneventfully for Kate. The service was to take place at six and therefore, after lunch, she spent a pleasant afternoon reading. Ellie took her for a walk in the grounds. A little way from the house she saw an imposing new pale brick building. Kate enquired what it was.

"Oh that is the Hall of Worship. You know, the Reverend Pike's place. Well, actually his house is nearby, there – you can just see it; it's called the Rectory, but I don't think there was ever a pastor here before Papa built the Hall for the Reverend and Mrs Pike only a few years ago. It's in the Gothic style, I think."

Indeed, Kate recognised the popular ecclesiastical style, but there was no spire, no crosses, indeed there were no external signs of the Christian religion whatsoever. It must be a very low church, she concluded. Just behind this modern building was a fine Regency house with some sort of long, low farm building hard by, a byre or stables, she guessed.

Kate tried to ask Ellie about the Lord's Handmaidens and the mysterious Reverend and Mrs Pike, but she was uncharacteristically evasive and would not be drawn,

"It's a sort of wonderful surprise, Miss Spencer. But everyone loves it. I did, I know."

The Young Governess ★ 71

* * *

As the weather was unreliable, Alice, Ellie and Kate were driven the short distance by coach. On the way, Alice Fordham had once more mentioned 'the little acceptance ceremony' in which all Handmaidens and Followers must participate. Kate tried to elicit more information, but the older woman merely gave her a serene smile and said, "My dear, it would spoil the surprise. You must wait and see!"

Ellie nodded vigorously and smiled.

"The Handmaidens will take care of you. They won't let you do anything wrong. Just do what they say, Miss Spencer, and you will fare very well, I assure you," explained the young girl earnestly.

Outside the Hall of Worship several more coaches were drawn up, and Kate recognised Mary Beveridge and one of the prettier housemaids from Walthrop; evidently they had walked. A line of attractive girls between the ages of fifteen and twenty and dressed in white, flowing cassocks greeted each new arrival and led them inside. These, Kate supposed, were the Handmaidens of the Lord.

They were apparently the last to arrive,

for the heavy oak doors were shut and bolted behind them. Kate paused and surveyed the interior. It was unlike any church that she had ever visited: more like a meeting hall than a place of worship. There were several rows of pews, it was true, but these were ornately carved and luxuriously upholstered in burgundy velvet; instead of an altar there was only a semi-circular dais with a lectern. At the back of the hall, by the entrance door, no font or organ could be seen, only a rather a curious arrangement of settees and *chaises-longues*, also upholstered in dark red crushed velvet. To left and right there were doors leading to smaller rooms, and it was to one of these, which appeared to be a vestry, that two smiling Handmaidens now led her to. As they parted, Alice Fordham gave Kate an encouraging kiss on the cheek and her arm a reassuring squeeze.

In the vestry two more Handmaidens greeted Kate with beatific smiles and now the oldest of the four whispered gently in her ear that they must help her to disrobe, so that they could dress her in the 'Supplicant's' robes for the ceremony. Kate began to be rather amused by the whole performance, which she found a little ridiculous, and happily entered into the spirit of the game, allowing the four girls' delicate hands to strip her naked. Then a simple calico apron or kilt was tied around her hips with a drawstring, only just covering her sex and her bottom. Over this a black velvet cassock was placed and she was led, barefoot, back to dais in the main body of the Hall.

Here there stood a tall, forbidding man, also dressed in purple ecclesiastical robes. Tall, slightly stooping and grey-haired, the Reverend Edgar Horace Pike had a long, horsey face with craggy eyebrows and abundant side-whiskers. He certainly looks the part of a man of the cloth, thought Kate. Even so, she noticed that the clergyman's solemn features had a sensual, somewhat dissolute cast to them.

The four Handmaidens brought her to a halt in front of an unusual piece of furniture that had replaced the lectern: a strange chair-like contraption similar to an elongated *prie-dieu*, made of carved oak and upholstered in red leather. As she turned to face the congregation she was surprised to see that it was composed solely of women, some young, some older. For the most part they looked like gentlewomen, well-dressed ladies of quality, perhaps a dozen or so. There was also a more humble contingent, servants such as Mrs Beveridge and the housemaid from Walthrop. To Kate's left, in the front pew, was a thin, fierce-looking woman in an old-fashioned coalscuttle bonnet, dressed entirely in a forbidding black. Her gimlet eyes also shone black and they seemed to penetrate and devour poor Kate's very soul as she stood there. Kate wondered, due to her placing in the Hall, whether she might not be the Reverend's wife. On the other side of the short aisle in the very front pew sat Alice and Ellie who both smiled at her encouragingly.

The Reverend Pike turned towards her with a benign, half-welcoming gesture, raising his beetling brows and baring his large, horse-like teeth. Kate smiled back nervously.

The Reverend surveyed his victim appreciatively. There had been so many lovely flowers, he thought, each one more rare than the last, it seemed, but this one... this gorgeously sublime creature surpassed all. He nearly laughed aloud as he thought of the sport Mrs Pike was going to have with her. Surely, his beloved wife's first thought when she saw her would be of the Punisher, that splendid instrument of pain and pleasure combined. He peered in his wife's direction and thought that he could detect the ghost of a smile play around her thin lips. As the Handmaidens led Kate to the *prie-dieu*, he smiled again and then he intoned in a loud, scrannel voice, "Divest the Supplicant of her outer raiment!"

Before Kate could fully comprehend the

enormity of what the Reverend Pike had just said, two Handmaidens had deftly removed her black cassock, and two more either side of her each firmly grasped an arm. Acutely aware that she was now the focus of attention, Kate blushed furiously. But for the little white cotton kilt, she was naked, only her sex hidden at the front and the lovely globes of her buttocks at the back. Kate stood, her superb breasts proud and naked in front of the small congregation of women. Never had she felt so very exposed, and she blushed continuously.

The Reverend Pike paused to watch the embarrassed, slightly awkward movements she made, the contours of her voluptuous body increasingly arousing the licentious excitement within him. In his debauched lifetime, he had never laid eyes on such perfect breasts... so pointed, full and erect, such erotic, pleasure-filled hips, such exquisite, perfectly formed thighs and legs... all these plus a face truly meant to excite the passions of a saint. Ah, that rosebud mouth, those small but sensuous lips, those serious grey eyes... what a rare, rare gem he had been granted! And how prettily she blushed!

"Let the Supplicant kneel and assume the position!"

Kate frowned in consternation, but she had no choice but to obey, and she knelt on the soft leather, her head pushed down by gently manoeuvring hands until she was helplessly thrusting her buttocks into the air behind her. She sensed the old man approach the *prie-dieu* and waited nervously.

"Handmaidens," he said commandingly, "lift the Supplicant's apron!"

Kate felt the two Handmaidens lift and fold back the little kilt so that her buttocks were completely exposed. This was the Reverend Pike, she thought bitterly, the man she had hoped would bring her comfort, spiritual advice and peace of mind.

Alice Fordham had betrayed her!

Pike knelt behind the naked young governess; the two Handmaidens tending to him parted his robes, and his erect, heavy cock heaved massively into view, pointing towards the crinkled, tan ring of Kate's anus so lusciously displayed to him between the full rounded spheres of her splayed buttocks. He leaned forward, probing his saliva-wet tongue upward from the moist flanges of her cunt-mouth, along the spread crevice to her tiny prune-wrinkled, hairless anus where he tried to penetrate with its stiffened tip, but the sphincter was too snug, too tight, and instead, he accomplished his main purpose... to lubricate it well.

Only Kate's eyes betrayed her, wide and staring straight ahead as she struggled to understand why she hadn't leapt to her feet to run as hard as she could through the door of the church.

Then, he raised, and taunted her cunt with the violent purple head of his prick, the foreskin peeled well back, until her whimpers drifted back to him. He insinuated its head between the moist split of her lips to gently tease her clitoris, and she commenced to moan incessantly and her cunt suddenly began to lubricate copiously. Her eyes half closed and her mouth fell open in pleasure.

Finally, he introduced the colossal, spongy glans into the viscous coated channel, never stopping, but continuing a constant penetration until its entirety was submerged in slow, tormenting inches into the very depths of her belly, and the half-dozen times she was about to cry out she held herself, not knowing why, only realizing that this devastating, constant plunge into her entrails was what she wanted, what she so desperately needed.

The massive head of this invading monster was slowly slipping into one of her body's deepest cavities... and she wanted it so. Suddenly, her own hand slipped between her thighs and spreading the soft curls of her pubic hair, caressed the erect bud of her throbbing clitoris. It caressed, stroked and taunted the already passion-inflamed nubbin as it pulsated lasciviously between her open legs.

Dear God, I want to die with this in me! thought Kate.

The Reverend Pike slowly withdrew his massive, hardened cock. He raised it until its unseeing eye was level with her hairless, puckered anus. He might have prepared it better by stretching it with his fingers, he thought wistfully, but some pleasures were better unannounced.

He doubted that she realized he was penetrating her brown star at first try. And then, she must have felt it prodding and working against her tight anus. She would have to decide it was much too big. She would judge that with certainty. He grinned to himself and wormed the tip of it into the snug, resisting little aperture. He could feel the foreskin being stretched back against his long, thick tool and he gave a quick hip-thrusting stab until he could feel it slowly slipping its way into her rectum. She would say to herself, it was all right... it was all right... because she could say nothing else... and by then, he would be well beyond the barrier of the clutching muscle.

His predictions were correct. As his cock ground its way into her nether channel, Kate was seduced by the delicious feelings that her highly sensitive anus gave to her and lulled into a sense of false security. But then, suddenly, without warning, she felt as if a telegraph pole was endeavouring to burst into her body!

She pulled away, but he held her fast and continued.

Her eyes focussed and, to Kate's acute embarrassment, met those of Ellie. The girl was obviously very excited, the expression she wore was one of great pleasure – a pleasure obviously derived from Kate's painful experience. The cruel little minx, she thought. Another member of the Fordham family I'll never trust. At that moment, her tormentor gave another massive thrust and his enormous shaft burrowed even deeper into her entrails.

"*Aaaaaaaggggghhhhhh...* God almighty! Noooo, nooo, *nooo!* It hurts!" she cried.

The Reverend Pike grinned excitedly. Silly girl! Of course it hurt. It was supposed to hurt. He signalled to the Handmaidens who quickly and expertly looped four straps over Kate's wrists and ankles. And then he simply rammed and thrust.

"God, Jesus! It's too *big!* It's going to kill me!" Kate screamed back at him through her tightly clenched teeth, no longer caring a jot what the 'congregation' might think.

But it was there, ever moving inward and now, with such limited powers of mobility, she couldn't hope to escape it. His thighs thrust

hers forward; his arms holding her hips back to his.

Dear Lord, I'm helpless! I can't move... I can't move... !

"Push back!" he commanded.

She could barely think, but she knew she must react to his words. Every way was pain and more pain. These was not the same sensations as she had experienced when Sir Bradley had penetrated her. She did... she pushed back and opened her arsehole that final quarter inch by deliberate effort because she had been ordered. It was as if she were taking a huge, unrelenting log inside her, stretching her buttocks wider and wider until she thought she would die. His vicious cock surged right into her rectum, solid and extremely painful, but finally better because she had absorbed it all.

"Oh, ohhh, ohhhh," she gasped.

Suddenly, Kate heard him croon with delight and gasp as he began to saw rhythmically and without the slightest mercy deep up into the soft confines of her back channel.

She dug her nails into her palms, bit at her lower lip, as slowly the pain eased a little, although it was still a mixture of hurtful discomfort and stimulation. She felt strangely wet between her buttocks, and also strangely ashamed. She was being sodomized and she knew it. Kate was not entirely naïve. Mrs Proctor had told her about such things. She tried to concentrate on this thought, but each time her concentrations were destroyed by a skin-splitting thrust which jolted her forward and made her squirm back onto his fleshy stem that was meting out the punishment. Abruptly, she commenced to sense a masochistic joy. The pain was weirdly pleasurable. Her helpless predicament, her exposure to the beady, lustful eyes of her audience... the strangeness of the ritual... all conspired to make this an extraordinarily lubricious experience. She realized she was heaving backwards to meet the forward thrust of his loins. And she was undulating her body and moving her buttocks in tiny circles. She had already begun to feel quite excited through the pain and she almost wished that she could reach under her and gently clasp at his swinging balls. She turned her face sideways just so that he could see the effect he was having on her.

Kneeling above her, The Reverend Pike watched the brownish skin of the little round hole draw back with his prick, clutching it as if it didn't want him to come out. At first, the pressure on his cock had been almost too much to bear, but now it was just tight and exhilarating, the type of squeeze that promised to draw the sperm right out of his duct with the ferocity of a geyser at every stroke.

He gaped at his fleshy, violent shaft disappearing between her smooth, white, gyrating buttocks with each thrust. It submerged until not even a half-inch of it showed, straining wildly in that tight, resistant passage, its bell-shaped, lust-bloated head reaching far into her soft quaking belly.

"Ooooohhhh, Oooohhhh," she groaned as his pelvis smacked loudly against the softness of her twin white buttocks. The rampaging instrument, buried to his balls, felt like the length of an axe haft in her near-ruptured anal sphincter. Dear God, she was hopelessly impaled!

The Reverend Pike's testicles ached and his prick cavorted as if it were spring-loaded each time he rammed into her, and now she was moaning and adding to his joy by the movement of her delicate rump and the hollowing of her back. He watched her beautiful profile as his lips bared back from his teeth in a silent snarl of lust. Her complexion was flushed a bright red, her head turning from side to side now, her long chestnut hair strewn down over her sweating forehead like a madwoman... and she was panting for more. She was his... completely his! A slave, submitting to him. He could do with her anything he liked... and he did, gouging his cock into her rectal passage and leaving it there, listening to her whine as he merely jostled his loins, moving it tantalizingly about with fiendish delight.

"Oh... yes, yes," she hissed. "Bugger me! *Bugger me!*"

The Reverend Pike leered to himself in his fanatical pleasure. It was time now. In a ferocious thrust he yet again plunged his cock until his grizzled pubic hair tickled her and his heavy balls slapped her vulval cleft.

"Are you content, my child?"

"Oh yes, Reverend, oh *yes!*" she groaned, a violent shudder rippling through her whole body as suddenly the path to a righteous orgasm was revealed to Kate, no longer a distant possibility, but an imminent certainty.

He withdrew his prick to the glans, then thrust it forward until his balls slapped heavily against the flowered split of her cunt in one long, slow stroke. His cock tingled; his hairy, dangling cod tightened around his heavy, sperm-laden balls that were suddenly alive with fire. He could come now whenever he chose and he wanted to feel that torrent of sperm surging into her beautiful governess's arse; dear Lord, how he loved these rituals!

Pike began to stroke ever more rapidly into her, hard and fast, battering her quivering buttocks with his hips. She felt the Handmaidens' fingers work diligently on her nipples and even dally with her clitoris. She moaned loudly with the pleasure-pain.

"Oh yes. Fuck your great cock into me! Ram it into me! Bugger me hard! Squirt your filthy seed into my bottom!" she wailed back at him in a near-hysterical voice.

Her sudden obscene response to his cruel sodomy drove the Reverend Pike on like an enraged satyr. He reached down and pulled her arse-cheeks wide apart, commencing to drive his pelvis into her soft, yielding buttocks with hard, vicious slaps that filled the room resoundingly and drew approving, conspiratorial glances among the congregation as they became aware of the impending crisis. Sweat from his face dripped into her lovely hollowing back, making it glisten. His breathing came in short puffing gasps like those of a tired oarsman, his vision locked on the whiteness of her quivering body that was slipping back over his plunging cock with the snugness of a velvet glove. Dear Lord, he was losing all control now as he sensed his great shaft growing unbelievably. His scrotum hung heavy with its bloated reservoir of sperm, and it must he emptied soon or burst from the excruciatingly delicious pressure.

Kate had fallen to mumbling unintelligibly beneath his pounding hips. She waggled her buttocks salaciously back against his merciless thrust. She wanted him to spend. She wanted him to squirt his heavy load of hot semen deep into her belly. She wanted him to split her crotch wide open and spill his sperm into her until she was completely immersed in its delicious loveliness. She could feel a sopping wetness in the crevice of her bottom and there was no longer any thought of pain, or of any other thing except this magnificent cock pummelling her battered arsehole. She pressed her shoulders to the upholstered leather so that her bottom was now raised even higher in the air, and the huge, frenzied cudgel could fuck into her at will. "Praise the Lord! It is time!" the Reverend Pike almost shouted in a harsh, booming voice, throwing back his head and groaning as he thrust his cock's full length into the wide-stretched opening to her bowels, his body commencing to jerk convulsively, his mouth falling open slackly as he clawed at her waist with harsh, clutching fingers, pulling her buttocks even wider apart for his prick to skewer yet another fraction of an inch into her.

"Thrust back! Thrust back!" he commanded her.

Kate, beneath his battering attack, thought she could feel the first delicious torrents of the hot, white cream splutter into the depths of her rectum. It surged through her body with the force of a bursting dam, burning into her heaving belly like hot, liquid fire. The delectable sensation touched off her own climax and she creamed as the vast gush of pleasure rippled through her, and then she could feel some of his warm sperm escape and dribble down the crevice of her wide-split bottom to the slit of her open, throbbing cunt... and then he was withdrawing his deflated member from inside her with a shamefully loud expulsion of wind that was followed by another little gush of viscid semen that spattered the leather upholstery below.

Slowly, Kate collapsed, every muscle in her spent body quivering from sheer exhaustion. She lay on her belly, and she turned and stared up in utter disbelief at this man who had somehow come to exercise this weird, unholy power over her senses. Now, in the wake of her played out passion, shame and revulsion inundated her, causing the tears to flow quietly from her eyes.

Dear God forgive me! I could not help myself. It was as if I had no control!

But she knew full well that once he had started, she wanted him to continue performing that bestial, forbidden act upon her. She knew that she was addicted to sexual congress of any sort, with any human being. Oh! What is to become of me now, she asked herself piteously.

The Reverend Pike came closer into her tear-blurred view. One of the Handmaidens was wiping at his penis with a small white towel. He was smiling... almost leering, Kate thought.

"Wipe away your tears, young lady," he said, giving her a ghastly grin. "You are now a Handmaiden. Tomorrow you shall become a Follower, a far more testing experience, I can assure you. And for heaven's sake, girl, a good fucking in the arse never hurt any female, nor is it anything to be ashamed of, if that is what your tears are about."

Kate clenched her eyes closed tightly, biting at her lower lip until she actually tasted her own blood, the filthy words sending a wave of nausea coursing through her. She had never felt so alone in her life. She was caught in an abominable trap and she didn't know how or why, or where she could turn. She couldn't go to Alice. Nor the Belfonts. Nor even Mrs Proctor. Not now... not after this! She had no one but herself to rely on. And it was this thought, far more than any other, she knew would sustain her through the trials that so clearly lay ahead. For what did the horse-faced cleric mean when he spoke of 'a far more testing experience'?

Gently, the Handmaidens led her back to the vestry where they bathed her with warm, scented water, washing away all traces of her ordeal and helped her to dress. In the coach, on the way back to the house, Kate answered

Alice and Ellie's solicitudes with sullen brevity, but she gave them no indication of her anger or desperation. She would find a way to leave the Fordhams of Walthrop. Somehow, she would. She *had* to!

Chapter Four

The next day Kate started her job in earnest. She was up early and by nine o'clock had breakfasted and put the neglected schoolroom back in good order. When Ellie appeared to take her first lesson, her new governess sat at a table with her back to the bow window appearing, or so she hoped, as forbidding as humanly possible.

Ellie was quite unprepared for the strictness of her lesson. To demonstrate a point, Kate would tap the end of her pencil on the wooden surface of the table, or if Ellie's attention wandered for a fraction of a second, she would slap down a thin wooden ruler with a fearsome 'crack'. In less than an hour, Kate had reduced her pupil to tears. Although she knew it was wrong to take it out on Ellie, and perhaps not very diplomatic, Kate found this was a small, but satisfying, recompense for her humiliation in front of her pupil, her mother and those dreadful women yesterday.

As Ellie, who was, in Kate's opinion, not one of Nature's natural scholars, struggled over her sums and her French irregular verbs, Kate had another chance to review her time at Walthrop. She had only been here a few days and already her world had been turned upside down. And this evening she would be subjected to another sexual ordeal at the Hall of Worship. She very much hoped that the detestable Reverend Pike would not be there.

* * *

While Kate was attempting to drum a few basic facts into poor Ellie's empty head, Sir Bradley and Lady Fordham were exchanging ideas of a very different nature in the conservatory. They were quite alone and talking most amiably.

"My dear Alice, I agree. She is a splendid fuck. Of course, I agree with you there. But we must ensure that my old friend Belfont never learns of her, ahem, *extra-curricular* activities here. If he or his wife ever found out we would have the dickens of a row on our hands. The scandal would ruin us."

His wife gave him a sardonic look.

"And what if she should fly the coop?"

"Why, m'dear, I have every confidence in your powers of, ah, *Lesbian* persuasion.

You are making her a 'Follower' tonight, are you not?"

Alice nodded.

"Well, if that doesn't break the filly, then we really shall have a problem on our hands."

"Leave it to me. She will be available for your 'guests' when they arrive later in the week. Even if I have to give her another of your Laudanum tinctures."

"Why did you not give her some before old Pike had his filthy way with her?"

His wife gave him a vulpine smile.

"Because I wanted our little trollop to feel it more keenly... and suffer. Ellie did. And so did I. And besides, through pain comes pleasure, as that old sodomite Pike and his bitch of a wife Bella are always so fond of pointing out. But tonight, have no fears, I will make sure she is well dosed."

"Can't stand that wretched couple. I feel quite sorry for poor Miss Spencer, really."

"I can't think of a better arrangement than that which we have now," replied his wife sharply. "Besides, who else could we possibly trust to take care of your little angels?"

* * *

That evening, Kate found herself once more seated opposite Alice and Ellie on the short coach ride to the Hall of Worship. She had promised herself that afternoon, to stage a last minute rebellion. To inform Alice that it was her time of the month. To plead temporary insanity. Anything! But after dinner and some more of the delicious, heady wine that she found so hard to resist, she had gone along meekly with them. After all, she reasoned to herself, she may as well get it over and done with. Then perhaps they would leave her alone.

The interior of the Hall was brightly illuminated by a myriad of lamps and candles and to Kate the effect seemed quite beautiful. Extravagant quantities of fresh flowers had been placed in great vases placed decoratively around the raised platform at the end of the Hall and their scent filled the large room. Again, there was the same number of women – about fifteen, thought Kate, not counting the Handmaidens – as the last time she was here. They were talking animatedly, but an expectant hush descended upon the company as the Walthrop party arrived and all eyes were upon Kate. Again, in the centre of the dais, sat that instrument of her last torture, the *prie-dieu*. The Handmaidens were much in evidence.

The woman who had been dressed entirely in black on her last visit came up to them. Now she wore ecclesiastical purple robes similar to those that the Reverend had worn on that occasion, and Kate realised that this must be Mrs Pike.

She addressed herself to Alice, however, not Kate.

"So, this is to be our new young Follower, Lady Fordham. Pretty. Very pretty."

She clapped her hands once and six nubile young beauties appeared.

"Handmaidens! Take her to be disrobed!"

Kate seemed to glide mysteriously from one situation to another with no conscious memory of the journey, as if her sense of time and space were slightly distorted; once more she found herself in the vestry. This time, however, the half-dozen, smiling, robed Handmaidens who undressed her were much freer with their delicately enquiring, busily delving and tweaking fingers. "How pretty she is!" Kate heard one half-whisper to one another, "See how ripe an' ready fer plucking!" "Blimey! fer *fucking*, don'tcher mean?" the other said, and the voices dissolved into more giggles. Such liberties they took, thought Kate vaguely. Her nipples were pinched into a state of reddened stiffness. Eager young hands cupped her breasts. Her pubic hair was fluffed and combed; her labia were squeezed and stroked, with special attention to the clitoris. Not even her pretty little bottom-hole was left in peace, as an oil-slick finger insinuated itself to the first knuckle there. Kate started to quiver and shake with the divine sensations induced by these mischievous, but tender, ministrations. She felt pleasantly light-headed, and seemed to drift in and out of a delicious warm and dreamlike state. Finally, rouge was applied to her cheeks and her nipples.

Suddenly Kate was aware that she was back in the hall, and the atmosphere had been transformed. Where she had left a gathering of respectably dressed young and middle-aged women, now a witches' coven existed. All were naked or nearly naked. All focussed their smiling attention on the youthful governess. She was led to the *prie-dieu* and bade to lie down, this time, on her back. A circle of predatory female faces looked down upon her and Kate felt scared. What did they want of her... surely not all of them were... lesbians!

The group parted to give a new arrival space. Like the others, Bella Pike was naked, but for a leather belt around her waist, from which dangled a fearsome device made of black India rubber and fashioned in the shape of an erect male member. In her drugged condition, certain details became almost preternaturally clear and now she could see that the shape of the phallus was more complex than she had thought. It was grooved in such a way that the ridges would give maximum sensation to its recipient. The scrawny cleric's wife stood at Kate's feet, looking down on her sacrificial lamb. Her dark, beady eyes glittered greedily. Kate noticed that her breasts drooped and that she had a little pot belly, below which grew an unruly mass of dark pubic hair. She spoke in a surprisingly deep, masculine voice. 'Bella' was perhaps a misnomer, however there was an undeniable aura of powerful sexuality about the woman, Kate thought.

"Tonight Katherine Spencer will be tried and tested by the company present for graduation from Handmaiden to Follower. She will join our sisterhood and taste the fruits of our love and desire. And she will give to each of us what we most desire of her. She is sworn to uphold our secret society. Under pain of death!"

"Under pain of death!" murmured the assembled women.

"Then let her trials begin..."

It started with the Handmaidens, who remained clothed in their white cassocks, adjusting Kate's thighs to expose her sex to its best advantage. This time, her torso was lower than her shoulders, so that her genitals were generously displayed. My cunt, she thought to herself, they're all looking at my cunt! She felt a sting on her breasts and saw that one of the Handmaidens, a pretty, big-breasted, redhead, was holding a flail with silken cords. She brought it down again and again, Kate felt the sting of the delicate silk fronds on her nipples. The sensation was wonderful, and it almost instantly triggered a shameless lust in her and she knew that she was getting wet, very wet indeed, between her thighs.

Her dark, intense eyes growing a little softer, Mrs Pike reached down to cup her hand over the curly mass of pubic hair between Kate's outstretched legs. The brunette gasped as the naked cleric's wife applied pressure with her bony fingers, then moved in slow sensuous circles, lovingly massaging the young woman's hairy, moistening cunt. The fact that yet another, unfamiliar female was touching her in such an intimate spot brought colour to Kate's cheeks. Suddenly she longed to touch her pendulous breasts, to feel the soft mounds of forbidden flesh under her fingers.

Moaning, Kate's hands reached up to cup the twin, dangling, pear-shaped breasts. The firm smooth flesh felt pleasant and Kate found her hands moving in slow sensuous circles. Almost as if they possessed a will of their own, her fingers kneaded the ivory, pink-tipped dugs, the delicate nipples tightened under Kate's attention and the excited governess let her fingers slide across the pink rosettes. Mrs Pike's stiff nubbins felt delightful under her fingers, and Kate was gratified by the way they rose in quick response. Eager to bring Mrs Pike still greater pleasure, she opened her hands to aim her palms at each distended nipple. Moving her hands in quick circles, she rubbed her palms across each fiery nub. She heard the older woman gasp, then felt her fingers move downwards to slip ever more deeply into the swollen folds of Kate's inner sex. Kate's legs trembled and she split them even further to accommodate Mrs Pike's busy, inquisitive fingers.

While the mistress of ceremonies fingered her throbbing cunt, a Follower, a slim, small-breasted, blonde woman reached from behind to seize Kate's generous breasts in her hands, kneading them vigorously, making her breath come in hot little gasps. Craning behind her, Kate could see her face; she saw that her eyes were glazed over with lust and the tip of a pink tongue had slipped out between her lips in a way that suggested pure erotic enjoyment. Kate abandoned the palming of Mrs Pike's distended nipples in order to reach upwards and grasp the newcomer's pert little breasts the way the Follower was grasping hers, good and hard. Whimpering, Kate squeezed the twin hills of flesh enthusiastically, her excitement mounting. She heard laughter and felt the lash of the flail on the inside of her thigh, but suddenly it did not matter who was laughing at her, or whipping her, or why.

Nothing mattered now except the wonderful way that Mrs Pike was exploring her throbbing cunt while the other woman played with her tits. The combined carnal treat, along with the thrilling experience of fondling another strange woman's breasts, was almost more than the excited girl could bear. Her heart pounded and her breathing grew ragged. She forgot everything but the frantic beat of her streaming cunt. The blonde Follower's fingers moved to her nipples, twisting and pinching the sensitive caps while Mrs Pike's fingers toyed with her oily slit. Finding the stiff bean of her clitoris, the gaunt woman squeezed and nipped it between her fingers. Kate's hips began to move in heated circles while catlike mewlings came from her throat. Encouraged, Mrs Pike flicked her forefinger back and forth across the fiery nub until Kate arched her back and cried out in an abrupt orgasm, her hands still spastically kneading the blonde's small breasts just as she was squeezing hers. The brusque climax she experienced took her almost by surprise. "Ahhh! I'm *spending!*" she cried in astonishment, her pelvis bucking.

It was only a beginning.

Mrs Pike took the Punisher from her belt and, fixing Kate with her glittering stare, beckoned a Handmaiden to her side.

"Lick this until it is well and truly ready for its purpose."

The Handmaiden, the redhead who had plied the whip, started to lick and suck the rubber dildo, coating it with her saliva. Kate did not have to use great powers of imagination to guess what its intended use was. The girl returned it to her mistress. Grasping the phallus firmly, Mrs Pike slid its shiny, spittle-slick head between the lips of Kate's sex. Kate wanted it. She thrust her hips forwards and upwards, and the head slipped into her vagina.

"Fuck me. *Fuck me with that thing!*" Kate heard someone say… unaware that the words had issued from her own mouth.

"Oh yes, my pretty one, we will. The Punisher and I will fuck you until you beg for mercy, then afterwards…"

Then, in amazement, Kate watched as her woman-lover stepped into an arrangement of fine leather straps that could effectively receive the black monster into place over her hips, causing the phallus to lance out from her loins in an almost realistic reproduction of a man's hardened cock.

She saw that its base was more or less flat and nestled in against Mrs Pike's vulva, making it look as though it belonged there. But it had to be said; there was a certain ludicrous appearance to the whole ensemble. The hard maleness of the artificial prick so suited the angular frame of the woman's body that it would have been laughable, had not Kate's need for sexual satisfaction been so real. There was no time to consider its more amusing aspects.

Now more for the effect than anything else, a grinning, strangely ithyphallic Bella Pike was sadistically thrusting that huge, substitute penis into the redheaded Handmaiden's mouth and halfway down her throat as the young girl knelt submissively before her. Next the cleric's wife turned and kneeling down herself, and positioning herself between Kate's legs, spread the girl's saliva along the enormous India rubber cock.

Unconsciously, she spread her thighs wider, expectantly, wanting it, now! Oh, God! This is wrong, but I don't care. But even in her mildly drugged state, Kate suspected that there was a condition attached to what Mrs Pike was doing for her. Afterwards! Oh, God! Afterwards, she had said... she must mean that I'll have to... let her use her... her sex... on *me!*

But that was in the future. For it was then she felt that huge substitute cock, as Mrs Pike guided it up and down the juicy furrow of her cunt, rubbing it against her throbbing clitoris.

"Oh God! Put it inside me! Shove it in!" she begged, lifting her churning hips up to it.

Kate could almost imagine that it was Sir

Bradley's massively stiffened penis that was going into her once again, to rob her once more of her maidenhead, as the scrawny woman wedged her hips down between the young governess's legs and guided the surrogate cock straight into her trembling, apprehensive vagina.

"Do you like that...?" she asked, gazing down impassively into the face of the girl she now pinned to the *prie-dieu*.

"*Ahhh!*" Kate moaned. "It'll tear me apart!"

As the dildo drove into her vaginal sheath, Kate vainly attempted to back away from it, its great girth stretching her cunt's mouth cruelly. God! It feels almost like the real thing! It wasn't, of course. Even a hardened prick is somewhat flexible, and there is that special heated warmth of its blood-engorged length, its throbbing heartbeat, its vibrant aliveness, which was missing from the rubber substitution; however, Kate closed her eyes, her imagination allowing her to believe that it was real... that it was Sir Bradley's penis that clove her cunt so effectively.

Above her Bella Pike began to flex her hips, imitating the fucking motions of a man. She smiled her own secret smile of triumph. Deep and hard, far up into the girl's seared vaginal tunnel, she continued to drive the rubber cock, while beneath her, moaning unceasingly, her hips undulating against the thrusting dildo, fucking back wildly, Kate was on a voyage of unexpected sexual delights.

"Oh, God! Drive it hard... and deep!" she whined pleadingly.

"OOOoooohhh ..."

Her words were stopped by Mrs Pike's mouth descending upon hers. Greedily, she accepted the other woman's warm wet tongue, sucking and nibbling on it wantonly, as it surged in and out of her mouth in imitation of the artificial fucking action below. Spurred on by her imploring cry, Bella Pike plunged the rubber cock in and out of the younger woman's cunt almost as wildly as a man might have done.

Kate's body responded wildly. Her eyes glazed and her breath was coming in rasping, laboured gasps now. In just a few moments, she knew that she would spend. God! It was going to be beautiful. Just as if a real man's penis were going in and out of me!

Suddenly, she convulsed, her climax breaking over her as if it were a great wave, her ecstatic body accepting it, revelling in it, enjoying every moment of its brief existence.

"Ohh!" she cried in rapturous joy. "Oh yes, *yes! I'm spending!*" Then in a full throated scream, she thrust her hips up hard against the pistoning rubber cock and released her pent-up sexual tension in blessed orgasm.

The shudders of her lovely body became less and less violent. Opening her eyes, she looked up into the dark, glittering depths of her seducer's eyes that watched her closely, and she was aware of the soft fullness of Mrs Pike's dangling breasts mashing down hard against her own firm orbs, now sprinkled with the sweat of her passion.

"You really enjoyed that, my girl didn't you... I fetched you, did I not?" she asked.

"Oh, *yes!*" Kate panted with rapturous enthusiasm. "You did, and it was wonderful."

"Well, now, it's my turn... and you must fetch me."

With swift expertness, Bella Pike shifted her body's position; she straddled Kate's face, her thighs spread wide, her head coming down naturally in a classic *soixante-neuf* position over the young governess's still quivering loins.

Kate was suddenly looking up, startled, into the moist, coral-pink cleft of Mrs Pike's demanding cunt. It hung there only inches above her face tantalizingly, and she could see the dense black forest of wiry pubic hair that surrounded it. Above the loose-hanging, lust-swollen lips, an unusually large clitoris had emerged from under its hood, throbbing with desire, while below the wrinkled brown expanse of her anus seemed to wink lewdly at her. The older woman's drooping inner lips dripped with the viscous exudate from the walls of her vagina, and Kate could see the pulsing contractions just inside the opening. Sweet Lord, thought Kate! She wants me to... to use my mouth on her, on this monstrous... *thing!*

A surprisingly agile, swivel-hipped wriggle brought Mrs Pike's hot, pulsating sex down against the young girl's face, as at the same time her mouth moved down to Kate's tender cunt below.

Kate felt like screaming, at first. She felt trapped... almost as though she would suffocate, but then she felt the flicking tongue on her own quivering clitoris, so sensitive and ready for renewed action. A moan of surrender and delighted sensuality escaped from her mouth, and without thinking, wanting to do it, now, as repayment, she probed out with her small, pink tongue experimentally. Unerringly, her tongue's tip found the throbbing head of the large, phallus-like clitoris and licked at it voraciously.

Dipping her searching tongue into the moist warmth of the woman's cunt-mouth, Kate discovered that its flavour was slightly pungent but not at all distasteful; then as she followed her older lover's lead, she became more bold, more dexterous in her sucking and licking. Mrs Pike's writhing hips pressed down against her face and the laboured breathing of the woman on top of her told the young governess that the other woman must be feeling the same things she felt; it was all so deliciously sensual: her arousal became complete in a matter of moments, ascending from a plateau to the highlands of imminent orgasm in a dizzying spiral of excitement. Dear Lord! Don't let it stop... ever!

Together, the two women mounted towards the heights of their ecstasy as tongues lashed and licked, hands roamed caressingly, and mouths gasped out soft little screams and moans of mutual joy.

Then, Kate was mumbling words up into the moistness of the other woman's cunt. "Oh, that is so wonderful! Don't stop! Please don't ever stop... licking me... like that!"

And, voice muffled from down between her thighs she heard Mrs Pike moaning, "Oh, merciful heavens, girl, you are a natural cunt-licker! More, more, do it *harder!*"

Mutually giving and receiving, limbs intertwined in the sixty-nine position, feasting on each other's cunts with licking, sucking mouths, drinking one another's juices, their bodies' sexual tensions built beyond reason, as electrifying sensations surged through them, the two women came to the apogee of sexual orgasm together.

Kate felt it begin for her in the long shuddering convulsions that shivered through her body deliciously, the intense climax causing her legs and pelvis to jerk spasmodically as wave after wave of welcome release surged through her for the second time within minutes. It was a symphonic rhapsody of sensuality, leaving her satisfied and relaxed, and she didn't recognize her own voice screaming an incoherent litany of obscenities...

Above her, and almost simultaneously, Bella Pike ground her demanding cunt down into the young teacher's face with wild abandon, her voice coming from down between the girl's thighs, muffled, as from a great distance announcing the arrival of her moment of rapture. "Oh oh my! I'm going to... *spend!* Now, now *now! Ahhhh!*"

Collapsing then, Bella Pike rolled from her topmost position and reversed her direction to stretch out beside her new, young conquest, clamping her soft mouth to Kate's in a long, probing kiss, holding her close until the last tiny shudders of her orgasm quivered through her body.

Kate kissed her back, her own arms going around the older woman to clamp their ecstatic, sweating bodies close together, and she tasted the essence of her own loins remaining moistly on the older woman's mouth.

The women surrounding them clapped

softly in appreciation. It had been, after all, a superb spectacle.

Bella Pike arose from the *prie-dieu*.

"Lady Fordham, Ellie, will you take your turn now?"

Alice answered for both of them.

"Thank you, Bella, but we prefer to wait. We will take our turn later."

Mrs Pike surveyed the group of expectant women. "Then I suggest that you other ladies take your pleasure with Miss Spencer now. She can service two of you at once, I'm sure. Can't you my dear?"

Kate was struck dumb. *All* of them?

But service them she did – over the next two hours. Her bed of lustful torment was adjusted so that it was easy for anyone to either kneel between Kate's legs or, if they preferred, bring their sex down on her mouth. Some used the Punisher on her, strapping on the dildo's harness and pushing it in and out of her by thrusts of their hips; others preferred to use it by hand. Some opted for a *soixante-neuf* position, while others merely availed themselves of her sex or her mouth. Mrs Beveridge was one of the latter and Kate watched as her grizzled cunt was lowered onto her mouth. She did her best for the woman who spent copiously. "Thank you, my dear girl," she muttered as she awkwardly disengaged herself, "I shall not forget this…

kindness!" The thin, flat-chested blonde who had so enjoyably tormented her breasts before, now returned for another bout, only this time she simply slid her sex back and forth over the painfully erect nipples of Kate's tender bosoms until she achieved her little crisis in that peculiar way.

Kate serviced them all: there were large women, small women, fat and thin; mothers and spinsters, highborn and servants. There were those who delighted in wresting from her yet another token of Kate's orgasmic passion, those who were only interested in using her lithe young body to achieve their own. Some were greedy for all of Kate's charms, others more fastidious and selective in their approach. Some were kindly and loving, others predatory and harsh. And finally it was the turn of Alice and Ellie,

As they approached the *prie-dieu*, Kate realised that they had purposely waited until the other women had used her, though why this should be, she could not guess. Her body gleamed in the hall's soft, golden light with sweat and the juices of the numerous lesbian couplings. She was utterly spent and used, her hair unruly and plastered to her face, her mouth bruised with the force of many long and passionate kisses, her breasts and nipples swollen and tender from prolonged mauling. The whole area between her thighs,

from anus to clitoris, was hypersensitive and the lightest touch, the softest exhalation even, could cause her to jerk and twitch in a sort of involuntary sexual spasm.

Grasping the Punisher, Alice brought it to where her daughter's fingers were already provocatively delving.

"Oh, Mama, what a pretty cunny she has, do you not think?"

So saying, Ellie removed her hand to allow her mother to slide the grooved dildo into her governess's cunt and nimbly straddled her upturned face. Once more Kate looked up to receive a descending vulva. When it came to pretty 'cunnies', Ellie's was, she thought, the prettiest she had seen that night: the delicately formed outer labia with their light covering of downy golden hairs; the neat little inner coral lips peeking out so impudently and leading to the sweetest little hood of an as-yet-unrevealed clitoris; at the base of a flat tummy she could see Ellie's soft powdery-blonde bush, and when Ellie raised a thigh to shift her position slightly, the delectable pinky-brown star of her anus. Ellie's cunt had a sweet, flowery aroma. Its juices were also sweet, and although Kate's tongue was weary from licking so many women, she redoubled her efforts so that she could taste more of the honeyed syrup that dripped down into her mouth.

The Young Governess

Alice's manipulations were deft and skilled. Working with the large black dildo, she knew just how to bring her young employee to the boil. While one hand worked the grooved rubber phallus in and out of Kate's vagina, the other retracted her clitoral cover, and she craned her neck down to lick the highly sensitized little organ.

And that was all that was required to send Kate over the top. She bucked and heaved, she moaned and squealed; yet Alice was merciless, keeping her lips sealed to the poor girl's clitoris, tonguing it all the while. Kate's limbs started to thrash spastically and her hips shivered and shook in a dance of agonising pleasure. It felt to her as if a great steel spring inside her that had been winding slowly had reached its breaking point and suddenly snapped. Kate shrieked with ecstasy and a great jet of ejaculate gushed from her cunt, striking Alice's face full on; she lapped up the clear nectar, swallowing as if it had been the finest vintage Tokay. Kate was blissfully unaware of her liquid tribute to Alice's tonguing, but a few of the ladies gathered around the little group murmured their appreciation. While Alice and the others dressed, she closed her eyes and fell into a dreamless slumber.

At last it was time to leave. The Handmaidens threw a thick, hooded, cloak over Kate's naked shoulders and drew it tight around her. She was then half-pushed, half-bundled into the carriage and they were soon back at Walthrop.

Chapter Five

When Kate failed to appear for breakfast that morning, Alice Fordham smiled. When an hour and a half later, Jenks reported to her that Miss Eleanor was still waiting in the schoolroom for Miss Spencer to appear, Lady Fordham's smile broadened. She asked him to fetch her husband.

A slumbering Kate was shaken awake by Mrs Beveridge and told to dress quickly as the Master and the Mistress were waiting for her in the drawing room.

Kate hurriedly dressed and, only half-awake, ran downstairs to meet her employers. This time, it was Sir Bradley Fordham who spoke to her first, and his voice was angry.

"Tell me Kate, how much do we pay you a week?"

"Sir Bradley, I'm most apologetic for my tardiness… it's just that with the Follower's ceremony of last night, I…"

The baronet cut her short.

"I'm not interested in what you get up

to at night, young Miss, I would like you to remind me of what salary we agreed to pay you."

"Th-thirty-five shillings a week, Sir. Just over ninety pounds a year."

"With full bed and board, moreover. Do you not sit at our table and do we not treat you as a member of our family?"

"Yes, Sir Bradley," Kate replied in a forlorn, barely audible voice.

"These are absurdly generous terms for one so inexperienced in her profession. And yet you have chosen to repay this generosity by your extreme tardiness and dilatory ways. We cannot afford to keep slovenly staff in luxury; there are many who would give an eye-tooth for your position. So what do you have to say for yourself?"

"I-I will try to make amends for my lateness, Sir. I shall be more punctual in future. And if there is any small way I can repay you for this misdemeanour…" A pallid Kate let her voice trail off and looked for support from Alice, though she was not really expecting any.

"As a matter of fact there is. For the next three days, during Royal Ascot week, the house will be very full of guests and their servants. We shall need all the bedrooms, and yours to boot. You will therefore share the work and accommodation of the Handmaidens for this period and in this way you will be furnished with a highly beneficial reminder of how those less fortunate than ourselves must live."

Inwardly, Kate heaved a sigh of relief. That could not be so bad. To endure a little more attention from the randy old goat of a pastor and his equally concupiscent wife... and besides, those girls seemed so gentle, so sweet. She would happily work beside them, and share their dormitory or wherever they slept.

"I would be happy to do this, Sir Bradley. It is the least..."

But he had already waved her away and turned his back on Kate to talk to his wife. Alice caught Kate's eye and said quietly over her husband's shoulder, "Go on, Kate, and hurry; you may pack a small valise with your night things to take with you. One of the housemaids will accompany you to the Rectory."

* * *

In under half an hour, they had reached the Rectory. Mrs Pike greeted Kate coolly and dismissed the servant.

"I am informed that you will be staying with us for three days and working as a Handmaiden."

Kate nodded.

"Well, you will need some training, I suppose," sighed Mrs Pike. "Our best girl, Molly, will show you what is expected of you."

She leaned out the window and rang a hand bell vigorously.

"But... but I have no idea what sort of work..."

"My dear, I am far too busy to explain!" Bella Pike interrupted Kate. "Let us just say that she will show you how to entertain the gentlemen who are visiting, either for the day, for the races, or staying at Walthrop with Sir Bradley and Lady Fordham for the duration of Royal Ascot. And here she is. Molly, this is Kate. I would like you to settle her in. Now, I must really go and see Cook about luncheon."

Kate recognised the strapping redheaded girl from last night. Two or three years younger than herself, no more. Huge-breasted, freckles on creamy skin. Hair the colour of a maple leaf in autumn. Here she seemed more confident, more her own woman, more on her own turf.

"We've plenty of time, Kate, the first customers isn't expected until about five o'clock." Molly had a soft, rural accent and a musical voice. "But they'll be here 'til eight, and mebbe there'll be plenty of them. Now take your things, if you please, and follow me."

Kate followed her guide along the path that led through the little back garden to a gate, and there in the shade of some large beeches, lay the Old Stables, a long, single-storied building with a pleasantly aged look to it. Inside, a dozen or more stalls for horses were ranged in a long row. The other Handmaidens were variously occupied in sweeping, needlework and preparing lunch on a long table at the far end of the room. Were it not for the fact that they were naked, save for their little calico aprons, it would have seemed an entirely natural scene. Kate's buxom companion stopped at one of the stalls, pushed the door open and pointed inside.

"Here you are, Kate. Not the luxury you'll have been accustomed to up at the big house, p'raps, but it's home for the likes of us. We eats at the long table down that end and at thissun there's a washroom and water-closets."

Kate stared stupidly at the pretty girl, not comprehending at first.

"You... you mean you... we... actually *sleep* here? *Here* in these *stables?*"

"Well of course we does, you silly girl. B'aint be no room for us nowhere else. And we works here, and all!"

"Work? What sort of work?" asked Kate with a sense of rising panic. In the corner of the stall there was a ticking *palliasse*, a small stool, and on the worn, wooden cobbled floor, a layer of clean straw.

"Why this is where they fucks us, girl. The swells. The toffs. The nobs. The *gentry*. In the arse or fanny, it doesn't really worry me. Long as I gets me grub and ale. The grub's good here, better'n the workhouse, and that's for sure. Oh, and sometimes they wants you to suck them off. I *likes* that! Especially when they comes on me tits!" Molly gave a filthy laugh and paused to lift and squeeze her outsized, melon-like breasts by way of demonstration, and then continued, in a more sober voice, "They're nice boys on the whole. Only one or two rotten apples among 'em and they soon gets told off by the others if they misbehaves, like."

"But don't the girls get with child?" was all that Kate could think of saying.

"Not often. Only one – Betty – and now she's got a nice life, married off to a local farmer's boy. Unless it's our safe time of the month or they agree to spend outside us, the men wear these fancy rubber things. Them's the rules, see?" said Molly, tapping her nose conspiratorially.

Kate did not see. What she had just heard amounted to yet another enormous, incomprehensible and outrageous affront to her person, her self-respect, her liberty, her very sanity. Surely... she could not be expected to...

Kate gave voice to her thoughts.

"Surely they don't expect *me* to..."

"But of *course* they expect you to, m'dear!" Molly interrupted. "And you'll be the toast o' the swells. They'll all want *you*. Purty new girl like you, talking posh, yes... lucky for us you'll only be staying with us for a day or two, otherwise us lot'd have no fun at all."

Molly paused and looked at Kate critically, head to one side.

"Some of the toffs like to have two girls to sport with. Now *you're* a partner I wouldn't say no to... I remembers you from last night -- and you're a bit of a goer if I remembers right!" And Molly laughed a low, musical laugh, but one that did nothing to raise Kate's spirits.

"But have none of you girls thought of going to the police? A justice of the peace? You... we... are being prostituted!"

"Old Dan Wiggins? He's a nice copper, true. He likes us girls. He has one of us every month, see? And we gets regular visits from the local magistrate too, and even the lord lieutenant, sometimes, though he's a bit past it now. No, Kate, we doesn't go to the authorities, they comes to *us!*"

Once more, it seemed to Kate, the Fordhams had betrayed her. Why, they were no better than white slavers! This was no club for decadent lesbians – this was a *brothel!* Now she was to be fucked by men for *money!* Complete strangers, men she would never see again! Kate's sense of outrage was almost total, but somewhere far at the back of her mind, a small, clear voice was trying to make itself heard. Here were men, and likely most were married, too. But not all of them would be cheating on their wives. Some would surely be bachelors. Toffs and swells, as Molly so eloquently put it... eligible bachelors in other words. Wait and see, Kate. Wait and see, said the little voice.

Molly interrupted her short reverie.

"Come and meet the other girls," she said.

* * *

Nervously, Kate prepared for her first 'customer'. With the limited resources available in the washroom, she ran a comb through her hair and applied a dab of cologne behind her ears and on the insides of her thighs as Molly had told her to. She was relieved that the girl seemed to like her so much, for she didn't think she would be able to survive the ordeal that lay ahead without such a staunch ally. Molly had told her much in the short hours they had spent together.

"The girls that Sir Bradley and old Pike

choose are mainly from the workhouses. Orphans or abandoned by their parents and suchlikes, they're only too keen to leave that horrible place. And those two have a knack for sniffing out the randy ones." She laughed. "There's never more than about half a dozen of us. When we comes of age, Sir Bradley helps us find work in London. Our Jenny, now, she comes back to visit us the other day in all her finery – she's still sweet on one of the girls here, see – and she earns a pretty penny I daresay. Heavens! The jewels and fur stole she sported alone must have cost a fortune!"

She paused to help herself to another large slice of game pie. Kate had to admit, if this luncheon was anything to go by, the food the girls were given was delicious and plentiful – none of them looked hungry, that was for sure.

"Now usually, we gets a gentleman mebbe once or twice a day. But then Sir Bradley has these weekend parties and the gentlemen staying are business or sportin' friends of his. They likes to use us a lot more. Ascot week… that begins tomorrow… why the place is swarmin' with swells. I serviced nigh on twenty in a day, last season!" Molly giggled. "It was a lark, I'll say! All of us girls in our stalls, busy fucking and shrieking … the toffs wandering up and down, you'll see – it'll be like that tomorrow, a regular party. When the weather's warm, we are to wear just our aprons as we are now, and no more. Mrs Pike's ever so strict about that. She'll whip a girl for less. But she's not a bad old cunt – although not all of the girls like to lick her fanny; she keeps an eye out for us. Oh Lor! Talk of the devil. Here comes the old baggage herself now!"

The subject of their discussion appeared, looking extremely self-important. She smiled approvingly at Kate and drew her and Molly aside, leaving the other girls to finish their lunch at the long refectory table.

"Lord Barchester and his French manservant, a deaf-mute, will be arriving shortly. You have time to finish your luncheon. He has requested your company and that of another girl, Molly. I suggest you choose Kate, for this would seem a perfect opportunity for you to introduce her to the way our girls are expected to work. He is a pleasant enough man and his servant – although it is highly irregular for one of our 'visitors' to be accompanied thus – should be no trouble at all."

When Kate emerged from the washroom, Molly and Lord Barchester, a handsome, burly man in his early thirties, were waiting for her, seated at the long refectory table. Kate felt a warming tingle when she saw the way his eyes moved over her body, lingering at the swelling peaks of her naked breasts and again at the little calico kilt that barely covered the most intimate parts of her body.

"You are even prettier and shapelier than Sir Bradley described you," he grinned, his rich baritone masculine voice sending tingles through Kate. "Come," he said, getting to his feet and placing his silk top hat and cane on one of the chairs, "Henri's already waiting for us in Molly's stall."

Molly wore the same little covering as Kate and the shortness of the skimpy garment exposed her long, willowy legs from the crotch to her toes as well as the bottom curves of her opulent arse. Her wondrously large breasts hung like ripe melons against her chest, the nipples temptingly hard and prominent, begging to be kissed and sucked.

Lord Barchester finished his drink and smiled.

"Sir, you must understand that I am quite unused to this sort of... I-I cannot say that I find my predicament... ," Kate struggled to justify her presence, to cling to some tattered shred of respectability at the same time as trying to quiet the rising excitement she felt when her eyes were drawn to the bulge in Lord Barchester's trousers.

"Don't be silly," he told her. "If that's the case, we'll soon show you the ropes, won't we, young Molly?" The peer grinned widely.

"Oh, that we will, M'lord," laughed Molly.

She took Kate's arm and they fell back, allowing their 'visitor' to get a little ahead of them.

"You're a lovely one, alright, I've not seen better," whispered Molly into Kate's ear. "I think we'll have a grand afternoon, to be sure. Last time old Vincent tipped me a whole sovreign! If you'll excuse my being so bold and blunt, Kate, I am glad you're here because Lord Barchester does so enjoy seeing a new girl getting fucked by his Henri. That'll put him in a capital mood. And young Henri," she laughed, "he may not say much but he knows how use that big cock of his; I've never had a bigger one inside me."

They arrived at Molly's stall and Kate, pale and shaking half with nervousness, half with aroused desire, peeked over the door. Two *palliasses* had been placed side by side to form a sort of double bed and the deaf-mute reclined on one of them, already naked and looking comfortable and relaxed. He was a handsome boy, thought Kate, not much older than me. As she was thinking this, his eyes met hers with a directness that was more self-assured than arrogant. When she saw the size of the tall, swarthy Frenchman's cock, she knew why. Kate sucked in her breath in startled, yet pleased surprise.

"My, but he is tremendous," she could not help gasping.

"Yes, he is," Lord Barchester agreed, "and he fucks like a champion too."

"Wait until you see the size of his balls," Molly whispered, her hand sliding lightly up and down and around the swelling cheeks of Kate's arse. "They're beautiful – just like big plums."

Kate's heart beat wildly and erratically as she looked again. Just as Molly said, his balls were huge and as she looked, his massive, uncircumcised cock started to rise from its supine position. Licking her suddenly dry lips, Kate saw that his tumescent prick, even half-erect, was nearly twice the length of Sir Bradley's or the Reverend Pike's when fully stiff.

"Looks as though Henri can smell a couple of hot, juicy cunts," Lord Barchester chuckled as the Frenchman grinned and grunted, his immense cock rising ever higher in little spasmodic jerks.

Kate was filled with a kind of electrified lust as she stared at the growth of the deaf mute's vast member. Her cunt felt as if it were going to explode as Molly's hand kneaded the resilient cheeks of her arse, her fingers gliding lightly over the swelling curves and tickling the moist, hairy furrow of her sex. Beside her, Lord Barchester took Kate's hand and placed it on his stiff, fiercely throbbing prick. Now Kate felt that she wanted to be fucked and sucked and violated in every way possible, so highly aroused were her emotions. And when Lord Barchester felt her fingers tighten and dig into his prick and felt her body begin to tremble, he smiled.

"I promise you, Henri will be a great asset to this fucking session. Let us join him now."

The three of them entered Molly's stall. Lord Barchester had paid a pretty penny for the two girls and, as usual, had paid even more for his manservant to be included in the games. For just this purpose he had reserved them for the whole day. Once there Kate and Molly quickly removed their little 'cache-sexes' and the young aristocrat quickly removed his clothing. Kate was almost overpowered by the sheer animal sensuality of Molly's voluptuous body, as she stood smiling at Kate, naked as the day she was born.

Kate's hot, fevered eyes moved from the stunning redhead to Lord Barchester's thick, hard erection as it angled up and out from his hairy belly. It made her mouth water and her cunt tingle.

"Kate, why don't you and Henri get better acquainted?" Lord Barchester said to the breathless, wide-eyed Kate. "Then we can all get together afterwards."

Kate sat on a low, three-legged stool and stared at the beautiful French deaf-mute, his tongue licking over his lips, and a look of acute, almost animal, sexual anxiety on his face as he sniffed the delicious aroma rising from between her legs, indeed from the very depths of her fast-lubricating cunt. Softly, with a hand that trembled slightly, Kate reached out to stroke his cheek. At the same time, she opened her thighs to him, lifting her apron and showing him her cunt. The Frenchman looked at her then at Lord Barchester and Molly.

"Go to Henri. Go Kate, go to him." Vincent Barchester spoke as if he were talking to his favourite dogs.

Kate's head swam and she felt her cunt contract furiously when she saw the young Frenchman's tremendous cudgel of a cock – now fully extended beneath his flat-muscled, hairy belly.

"Go on, Kate, he won't bite," Molly called to her. "Play with him. He loves to have someone to sport with his cock. Go on, give it a squeeze. It's a beauty, is it not?"

Sliding off the stool, Kate knelt beside Henri in the clean straw. Her hand reached up under him to touch, lightly caress and then hold that fantastically hard prick in her hand. She felt it swell as her fist moved slowly along its thick warm length. It was greater, thicker and longer than she thought any cock could ever be. It was a prick that any man would be proud to own.

Shaking with pure sensual delight, Kate looked up at Vincent Barchester and Molly as they watched her and the handsome young Frenchman. Lord Barchester moved behind Molly, his cock sticking between her legs, that purplish knob thick and swollen as it protruded out from under Molly's pink-lipped cunt. Molly bent forward just a bit and Lord Barchester bent his knees, guiding the head of his cock up and into Molly's juice-dripping fanny. It was evident from the ease with which they established their connection, that they had done this many times before. He straightened up slowly, forcing more and more of his cock into Molly until it was buried to the balls in her fat, pink-lipped slit. Gripping Molly by the tits, he began to fuck her with fast, deep thrusts, his eyes as well as Molly's fastened on Kate playing with Henri's outrageously large cock.

Molly, her body angled slightly forward, her arms tight around her partners as they encircled her waist, responded to Lord Barchester's fucking with equally wild backward thrusts of her hips. She twisted her arse and ground it frantically as Lord Barchester jammed the full length of his long thick prick deep into her with each violent plunge of his hips. Suddenly he stiffened, deep rasping groans coming from him as he drove his shaft as far up into Molly's cunt as he could, then as Molly gasped, his body shook. Utterly fascinated and aroused, Kate looked on as the thick white juices dripped out of Molly's widely stretched cunt, and as she watched, her loins quivered and she almost came herself.

When Lord Barchester pulled his soft, limp, sperm- and juice-covered prick out of Molly's snatch, the flood of their combined loads poured out of her cunt in a little stream and trickled down the soft insides of her thighs. Excusing herself, Molly left to go out to clean herself up. When she had gone, Lord Barchester came over and knelt beside Kate.

"I'm sorry but I got so excited watching you fool around with Henri's cock, I just had to do something to get rid of the spunk I had in my balls. Kate, I know this will sound a little strange to you but I would like you to give Molly's cunt a good gamming."

"You mean, kiss and lick her fanny?"

"Exactly. She loves to be gammed by another woman. She likes you and would love it if you did that to her and made her spend."

"I'll be happy to," Kate agreed, excited

even more by the prospect of sucking the beautiful Molly's cunt. "But just please let me have Henri gam my cunt first," she said, a little unsure of this new terminology. "I'm just wild for it and can't wait to feel his tongue on and in my cunt."

"Certainly. You go right ahead and you'll get the tongue lapping of your life."

Laying back, Kate spread her legs apart, her fanny mouth opening wide.

"Suck, Henri. Suck me," she whispered throatily to the Frenchman, even though she knew he could not hear her, looking into his beautiful deep brown eyes. "Lick my cunt. Oh place your lips on my cunt and suck me…"

The Frenchman moved up between her legs and she trembled violently when she felt and heard him sniff at her dripping wet cunt. Kate cried out, her body arching as the Frenchman's tongue lapped at her twat with long, rapid licking motions. She could feel the pubic hairs around her cunt being matted flat at the Frenchman lapped avidly at her pulsating, pink-lipped gash.

Kate cried out with delighted desire as the Frenchman parted her labia with a strong, active tongue and started to lick furiously at her cunt. Reaching down she helped him by holding open the soft folds of her cunt-mouth. A low cry of sheer rapture came from her when she felt that acutely sensitive flesh being serviced by his deliciously agile tongue. Her body arched and jerked when it penetrated deeper than she would have thought possible. He created such exquisite pleasure with his few inches of muscled flesh that Kate wondered what he could do with that altogether larger part of his sexual anatomy that she was sure shook and quivered between his thighs. Henri tensed and flicked his tongue back and forth across her clitoris then dived down to the pucker of her little brown anus. He could make his tongue broad or pointed, it could delve or tickle and she felt their combined fluids drip down to the split of her buttocks. She was tremendously excited now, her hips bucking and humping as she was caught up in the swirling world of furious and overpowering lustful desires. A scream ripped from her and she twisted and squirmed as her body was assaulted by wave after wave of the most intense pleasure.

After the powerful spasms had ebbed, Kate collapsed on the floor as Henri licked up her flowing juices. Turning her head she saw Molly standing there, staring at her, a look of highly aroused sensuality on her pretty face. Oddly enough, Kate felt a reawakening of a new desire as she looked at Molly's beautiful, creamy-skinned body. Her hips swayed sensuously, her hard-nippled tits bounced thrillingly as she came over to Kate.

"Oh, Kate, you have such a lovely body," Molly whispered, her breath coming in short, hard gasps. "A real woman you are, so shapely and so sweet. Did you enjoy having Henri lick your fanny, Kate? I love having him do mine. But I'd like you to lick it even better."

Kate's blood raced at the erotic invitation in Molly's smouldering eyes and husky voice. She dropped her eyes to that copper-fleeced slit, seeing the soft, serpentine, coral pink lips peeking through the reddish-gold covering of silky hair. Unconsciously Kate's hips began to undulate and lift and fall not wanting Henri to stop that wonderful, sensual licking of her fanny. She was so hot and bothered, so furiously excited that she breathed heavily, almost panted, without knowing it.

"Why don't you come over here?" Kate husked, staring into Molly's eyes, her mouth open in the shape of a half-fulfilled kiss. "Come down with me and I will love that dear, delectable fanny of yours." She smiled archly. "If you would permit me to, that is?"

"Oh, yes, yes, yes," Molly groaned sinking to her knees in front of the panting Kate. Raising herself slightly she spread her legs wide and straddled the little milking stool, her wet juicy twat poised directly over Kate's head.

Looking up, Kate felt a surge of need and voluptuousness seize her at the sight of the aroused, glistening maw of Molly's luscious fanny. Her senses were aflame with a driving desire and her mouth filled with saliva as Molly lowered that delectable looking cunt slowly down to her reaching mouth.

Yet again, the young governess found herself wondering if she were not truly more attracted to her own sex. There was no doubt that she was tremendously excited and oddly stimulated by the almost overpowering musky odour of Molly's hot wet cunt, by the sight of those puffy lips opening like some beautiful, exotic hothouse flower as she touched them with the tip of her tongue. The taste of those salty sweet cunt juices ignited Kate's sexual impulses. Her tongue slid along those warm, spongy lips, then when Molly reached between her thighs to pull open that thrilling cunt mouth, Kate plunged her tongue deep into the hot warm recesses of the redhead's sweet tasting cunt, licking and lapping voraciously at that slippery cavern of delight.

As Kate poked and licked her tongue deep within Molly's twitching cunt, she thrilled to the thought that only a few moments before, Lord Barchester's manly prick had plumbed its very depths, before shooting his thick manly spunk inside. Indeed she believed she could detect the residual traces of his sperm in the plentiful juices that continually filled her mouth. Kate's lips closed hard around the redhead's thick, hard clitoris. The sounds of soft, sobbing cries, the jerking undulating of Molly's hips and the taste of those flowing cunt juices had Kate lost in a sea of raw, unequivocal, lesbian lust.

She fucked the randy girl's twat with her tongue using it as if it were a cock, thrusting and darting in and out, flicking hard across Molly's elongated, pulsing clitoris, feeling it throb between her lips as she sucked hungrily on it. The feel and taste of Molly's sex, hearing the harsh, guttural cries of ecstasy the strangled moans of pleasure inflamed Kate's own lust more than ever.

The way her head was bent back, Kate could see Lord Barchester. He was standing there and Kate's heart hammered when she was shocked to see Henri standing in front of him, avidly licking his master's stiff swollen prick. There was no doubt that the French manservant's tongue was having the same erotic effect on Lord Barchester as it had when he had gammed her.

Her breath burned in her throat when she saw Lord Barchester's knees bend and his burly body stiffen. His hand held his leaping pulsating prick, his face contorted with sexual strain as the long, clever tongue of the Frenchman licked faster and more furiously at the swollen red knob and the shaft behind it.

Lord Barchester's eyes were fastened on the two women as Kate's wild cunt-lapping was inspired by the bizarre sight in front of her. Molly's hips undulated faster and harder now as she mashed her wet cunt down harder against Kate's sucking, licking mouth.

A wild, almost animal cry came from Lord Barchester, forcing Kate to turn and once more look at the bizarre coupling. She was just in time. Lord Barchester gave a gasping cry of agonized rapture, his entire body stiffening and Kate's eyes opened wide when she saw the thick heavy creamy white sperm shoot fiercely out of the reddened glans of his taut-skinned cock to spatter on the straw-strewn floor. The first spurt went halfway across the room over the Frenchman's head, each spurt falling lower and lower until one long stringy drop slipped from the tip of his prick.

It was the first time Kate had ever seen a man spend from having his cock sucked and licked to ejaculation and the weirdness of it, the wild erotic shock triggered off another cunt rending orgasm in her.

As her furious spasms died, Kate could feel Molly's body tremble, her cunt rolling back and forth across Kate's mouth as the big-breasted redhead went wild, also affected by the bizarre spectacle of Lord Barchester made to spend by the Frenchman's tongue.

Kate could feel her cunt contracting fiercely around her tongue as she spent.

Opening her mouth wide, Kate sucked in and swallowed the sweet tasting elixir that ran down from Molly's fanny. Her throat gulped furiously as that sweet, warm sticky stream flowed down into her mouth.

Feeling Molly pull up and off of her, Kate looked up. There was a look of something more than violent sexual arousal on Molly's face. So moved was she by the experience of Kate's lovemaking that she was actually crying with lust and emotion.

"I want to suck and tongue and gam you," she sobbed. "I want to suck your cunt. Please. Let me gam your fanny."

Kate lay on one of the thin mattresses while Molly arranged herself above her in classic *soixante-neuf* position. Kate could feel soft, warm, slightly moist lips kissing and sucking gently on her cunt lips, driving Kate to a high pitch of sexuality. The almost hungry lapping of Molly's lips and tongue at her juicy fanny only made Kate hornier. Reaching up to hold the other's bucking hips, she rubbed her hands across the smooth cheeks of Molly's creamy, rolling arse as Molly licked sucked and tongued voraciously, uttering unintelligible sounds mingled with the slurping sounds of raw lust, her tongue lavishing exquisite sensations on Kate's tender gash.

Suddenly, Kate felt Molly lift herself off and before she knew what was happening, felt herself turned over on her stomach. Kate's body jerked in erotic shock when she felt Molly part the cheeks of her arse then insert her stiffened tongue deep into Kate's critically sensitive arsehole. She licked up and down the inside of Kate's thighs then flipped Kate over onto her back again, panting and moaning as she licked at the hot juiciness of the stable's newest recruit.

"Ohhh... I loves gamming a nice hot sweet-tasting fanny," Molly gasped, almost tearfully, her fingers digging deep inside Kate's vagina, rubbing her blood engorged tender clitoris excitingly with hard rolling, pinching and pulling actions. "I want to eat and eat and suck your juicy pretty fanny and make you spend in my mouth. Oh, it is such a beautiful cunt. So nice and pink and wet. Oh, Kate my darling, *now!* I'm going to *sp-spend!*"

Kate held the passionate younger girl tight, feeling her quiver and then tense, shaking and shuddering as she came. Her body trembled wildly as the involuntary spasms seized her, then with a weak, quavering gasp she relaxed, rolling off Kate and onto her side. Kate was surprised: she realised that Molly had achieved her climax even though she had not even had a chance to repay the redhead's ardent oral kisses. How curious, she thought: even though Molly was sucking me, it was she who spent, not I.

Kate, her own desires and passion now fully reawakened, though unfulfilled, lay there breathing hard. Her eyes lifted to look at the Frenchman who had silently watched the entire erotic episode with Molly. Now he lay close to them on the other thin mattress and Kate looked on as he slowly jerked his furiously swollen phallus. The way he gazed intently, pleadingly into her eyes, the way the foreskin moved on and off the gigantic purplish-red head of his uncircumcised cock as he worked his surprisingly delicate fingers up and down its huge shaft, all conspired to inflame and excite the very core of Kate's libido. When Molly got up and went to refresh herself in the washroom, Kate turned towards him, lying on her front and raised herself up, cupping her chin in her hands. Vincent Barchester looked on as he lounged by the door of the stall.

Kate instinctively knew what she had to do now. Jumping up and going over to kneel beside him, she ran one hand back and forth across that hot throbbing steel-hard prick, while her other cupped and fondled his huge balls. With the desire to feel this rigid huge shaft in her cunt, Kate knelt in front of him on her hands and knees.

"Fuck me, Henri. Fuck me. Mount me and put your cock in me and fuck me like the bitch that I am, a young bitch in heat. Get up and put that big Frenchie's prick of yours in my cunt. Oh Henri. Fuck me... fuck me... but don't spend inside me... I don't wish to be with child! *J'ai creinte de devenir enceinte*," she mouthed at him in her schoolmistress French. To her relief, Henri was able to read her lips and understood. He smiled and nodded reassuringly.

She tensed when she felt the handsome Frenchman mount her from behind, his long, muscular arms locking around her middle. Kate could feel the rubbery head of his enormous prick probing to find her open slit. A long shaking ecstatic cry of sheer bliss rose in her throat when she felt the entire length of that beautiful, thick, steel-hard prick jam into her with one thrusting motion. His balls were already swollen and his hairy scrotal sack was tight around the end of his shaft , adding to the sensations, the exquisite friction, that created unprecedented thrills for Kate as Lord Barchester's manservant began to fuck her in earnest.

She gloried in the fantastic feelings that flooded her as the deaf-mute fucked her with long, powerful, incredibly fast strokes that drove the head of his cock deep into the innermost recesses of her clinging, clasping cunt. It was unlike any other fucking she had ever had. The man's prick was fully as thick but longer than Sir Bradley's. Moreover he fucked her at a pace that, had it been the baronet's, he would have spent within a few minutes. Yet the Frenchman just went on and on, the tempo and rhythm of his rapid in and out thrusts never slacking or slowing.

Moaning and sobbing with sheer nerve tingling delight, Kate reveled in the perverse excitement of being fucked by this virile young man in front of his older master. She held her hips and bottom motionless as the Frenchman fucked her skillfully and expertly, burying the full length of his phenomenal prick, that incredibly stiff shaft, deeper and harder into her at a fantastic speed. The feel of his huge ball sac rubbing against the swollen split of her cuntlips had Kate sobbing with delighted rapture.

Looking up through lust-fogged eyes, she saw Molly and Lord Barchester staring wide-eyed at her being screwed. Molly had Lord Barchester's huge erection in her hand, jerking him off with slow steady strokes.

"Look at him go," Molly gasped excitedly. "Look at him fuck her sweet little fanny. Oh Vincent, my darling, let me suck your cock or fuck me while we watch Henri fuck that beautiful cunt."

Molly sank to her knees in front of Lord

Barchester, turning him sideways so they could both watch the Frenchman screwing Kate. Her mouth opened wide to encompass the thick swollen knob on the end of Lord Barchester's prick. Her hands gripped him by the cheeks of his arse, pulling him closer as her mouth slid back and forth along that thick veined cock.

"How... long... can... he... fuck?" Kate gasped.

"That rascal can go on for about twenty or twenty five minutes," Lord Barchester grunted, his body jerking as Molly sucked on his prick. "Once he fucked Molly for thirty five minutes."

"I... don't... think... I... can... take... much... more. His cock... it's so... big... it's... wearing... out my... cunt."

"Don't worry," Lord Barchester gasped, his hands gripping Molly's bobbing head. "I can tell that it won't be long before he finishes."

The Frenchman's prick seemed to grow even thicker and longer, his in-and-out strokes getting faster and Kate, who had already spent several times, could feel a massive orgasm, a truly great one, building up inside her stretched fanny.

With a growling, rasping sound, the Frenchman buried his immense prick to the very end in her cunt. A broken wailing cry came from Kate when her epic orgasm finally burst. Her body was wracked by fearsome spasms as the savage contractions of her cunt sent the most agonizing thrills through her. True to his word, the Frenchman wrenched his cock from the clasping confines of her sex and spurted again and again, his semen splattering the entire length of her shuddering, rippling, sweat-shining back.

She could feel each spurt of the Frenchman's scalding spunk on her back as if it were the delicious lash of a silken whip; his huge, slowly softening cock still twitched as it drained the remaining drops of his heavy, sperm-laden balls onto her sensitive skin. Kate fell forward on the floor, almost unconscious but thoroughly satiated by the tremendous fucking she had just received.

Hearing the wet slurping sounds of Molly actively sucking Lord Barchester off caused Kate to look around just as Lord Barchester stiffened and a string of lustful obscenities poured from him as he came. Just as he did, Molly pulled her mouth off his pulsating shaft and leaned back so that his thick white spunk splattered all over her heaving stiff-nippled breasts.

Transfixed, Kate gaped wide-eyed as the excitedly moving Molly's hand smeared Lord Barchester's spunk all over her tits, one of her hands spreading the thick cream all over those swollen mounds and especially around the thick erect nipples while she frigged herself energetically with the other. A low sobbing scream rose from Molly's throat and her body shook as she experienced another shattering spend.

Later, when they had all recovered, Lord Barchester suggested a drink for them all. He produced a silver flask of brandy and poured a large measure of the restoring spirit into small silver cups which he handed to each of them.

The wanton Molly smiled and turned to Kate as she wiped Lord Barchester's spunk off her tits with her fingers, then licked each one clean in turn. "Did you enjoy getting fucked by Henri, Kate? Isn't he a caution, just? That prick of his! Did he fetch you well and good?"

"It was out of this world," Kate replied fervently. "I've never been so beautifully fucked before."

"Then here's a toast to fucking and sucking," Molly proposed. "To the beautiful Frenchman who sucks and fucks cunts so well and to Lord Barchester's cock that tastes so good."

"I'll drink to that," said Lord Barchester wearily, but happily, raising the flask to his lips and draining the remainder in one long, gulping draught.

Kate swallowed her drink thirstily even though it burned her throat. The entire experience of having had Henri lick her cunt, of Molly eating her fanny, and vice versa, plus the unbelievable fucking she had just gotten, had exhausted her. Sipping what remained of her brandy, she replaced her calico apron and, after kissing each of the company, returned to her own stall and lay down to rest, contemplating all that had happened in the last few days. Soon she fell asleep.

There were no more visitors that day and when Kate awoke, she helped the Handmaidens in their more menial tasks. She enjoyed talking to the girls: Molly, her new friend, and happy as a girl could be, for Vincent Barchester had tipped her another sovereign; Meg, a pert little street urchin from Rotherhithe with a mouth as foul as any bargee; Annie, a jolly, bouncy, seventeen-year-old lass from Lancashire; Susan, an astonishingly pretty, waif-like blonde whose willowy looks belied a character tougher than nails, and Bessie, an Irish girl who at first viewed Kate with suspicion but soon became a fast friend with all the Celtic warmth and whimsicality of her race. Finally there was Ruth. Ruth was just sixteen, a sloe-eyed beauty, the daughter of an immigrant tailor and his wife who had died of cholera in one of the recent epidemics. Despite her relative youth, in Ruth Kate found a kindred spirit, and she could not help but make comparisons between this girl and another sixteen-year-old: the far less intelligent, but amiable, Ellie. After supper she felt tired once more and was quite happy to return to her stall and fall into a deep, satisfying slumber.

* * *

Next morning, the girls were up early, ready and available. Kate had awoken refreshed and with a more positive outlook on the ordeal that she had so feared to begin with; indeed, it was becoming more like a visit to some erotic paradise. She ate a hearty breakfast. At eleven o' clock, the first visitors started to arrive at the Stables.

Her first 'visitor' was a pleasant enough man. Reasonably good-looking and young enough to be her elder brother, his only shortcomings were the less-than-impressive size of his penis and the wedding band that he wore. There was little in the way of conversation between them. Since she was now quite certain that she was at a safe stage of her cycle, Kate allowed him to fuck her without a prophylactic, and relished the feeling of his pounding cock as it stiffened within her tight, juicy cunt and started to pulse its passionate emission into the depths

of her sex. She herself found that she was unable to spend, although the sensations thus generated were most enjoyable. The news soon spread that 'the new gal' was pretty as a picture, well spoken and fucked like a Whitechapel whore. Within ten minutes another had taken his place and thereafter she scarcely had time even to wash herself between fucks. Still, she failed to reach a satisfying climax. By lunchtime she had had seven more 'customers' and her near-virginal cunt was awash with sperm. The pretty young governess had also sucked her first man to spending in her mouth. The taste was not quite as bad as she had expected it to be.

There was a long lull during the period of luncheon and then the men started to arrive at the Stables once more. Molly's prediction of Kate becoming 'toast of the swells' proved to be correct. Indeed, Kate soon became so much in demand by the top-hatted, aristocratic, moustachioed gentlemen that a sort of informal queue formed, the men chatting amongst themselves in a clubbish sort of way and looking on in amusement while they awaited their turn with 'the new young filly'. Many did not even bother to undress, but simply unbuttoned themselves and took her while still fully clothed. Despite her efforts to enjoy being the centre of so much attention, Kate began to find their lack of imagination and finesse more irksome than exciting. There was no time to enjoy the individuality of each man, nor any time to find pleasure in these rapid, peremptory couplings.

Towards the end of the day however, after a longish quiet period, a man entered Kate's stall and asked politely if he could 'avail himself of her bottom'. As an antidote to the parade of uninspiring copulative experiences she had endured that long day, Kate consented almost eagerly. Suitably lubricated with finger and tongue, as well as a little oil that had been provided for that very purpose, the pretty governess quickly scrambled to a kneeling position with her buttocks high in the air and braced herself for what she hoped would be a pleasurable assault on her nether hole. Not entirely to her surprise, the experience was so much all she hoped it would be that she was quickly transported to a plateau of sensual delight and then, when her imaginative sodomite used his skilful fingers upon her responsive little nub, he contrived to bring her off so violently that she scared the poor man half to death with her joyful shrieks and brought her new-found sisters running to her stall in alarm. All was well, however, that ended well, with little Meg squatting down behind her hero and administering such an enjoyable tonguing to his own bottom, interspersed with the most foul-mouthed commentary on the act that he had ever, or was ever, likely to hear, that he was able to continue to the natural conclusion of his buggery: he fairly exploded into the very depths of Kate's rectum.

Chapter Six

On the morning of her last day as a provisional Handmaiden, Kate looked forward to the day with mixed feelings. On the one hand, she revelled in her newfound sensuality and her proficiency as a courtesan; moreover, she heartily enjoyed the camaraderie of her Handmaiden sisters. But equally, she began to wonder where all this would lead. Although she looked forward to returning to the certainties of her life as governess at Walthrop, her position there seemed insecure and fraught with dangers. A practical girl at heart, she realised that she was no nearer to her goal of finding a suitable mate for matrimony. She realised, too, that she still lacked the experience to venture out into the wide world without more than a few pounds to her name.

The answer to her dilemma came in the shape of a tall, sartorially elegant, dark stranger. Kate could not help herself: as the good-looking young man walked towards her, his handsome features were so genial and so full of good humour that she found herself smiling despite her gloomy musings.

"Miss Spencer, I believe?" he said.

Kate was covered in confusion. How could he possibly know my name, she wondered? Suddenly she felt very under-dressed in her little calico apron, and in a fit of irrational modesty, she had an almost unbearable desire to cover her breasts.

"To whom do I owe the pleasure, Sir?" she asked, blushing furiously and resisting the impulse to bring her hands up in order to shield her vulnerable bosom.

"I beg your pardon, Miss. My name is Robert Harcourt. I am Lady Fordham's brother, and to me has fallen the happy duty of escorting you back to Walthrop."

Despite her surprise at this news, Kate's eyes could not withstand the temptation of looking at Mr Harcourt's groin: here she saw an impressive bulge that seemed to grow as she watched. Tearing her eyes away, she drew herself up to her full height and, breasts proudly out-thrust, said, "Very well, Sir. I shall prepare to leave."

Just at that moment, Mrs Pike, a very

humble and ingratiating Mrs Pike, arrived with Kate's clothes.

"Here you are my dear. I'm so sorry, I was to have given you these earlier, before... before Mr. Harcourt arrived here. It seems that your time with the Handmaidens is over. We shall all miss you until your return, which we hope will be very soon."

Kate accepted the small bundle with a murmured thanks and went to her stall to dress. When she emerged, the transformation from *fille de joie* to demure governess was complete.

* * *

As they walked slowly back to Walthrop, Kate gave her saviour a sidelong glance. He really was very handsome indeed, she thought. Colouring a little, but taking her courage in both hands, she asked him, "Why has your sister decided that I may return?"

It was Robert Harcourt's turn to look uncomfortable.

"Oh," he replied vaguely, "I believe that my young niece was made inconsolable by your absence."

They walked on in silence for a few moments. And then he quickly overtook Kate, standing in front of her and seizing both her hands in his, letting her valise fall to the grassy path.

"No, Kate, if I may be so bold as to call you thus, the truth is that I begged my sister to be allowed to rescue from your terrible ordeal. You did not see me but I was there... there in the Old Stables, yesterday. I saw how... how they *used* you... it was..."

His earnest voice died to a whisper and he found himself at a loss for the right words.

Kate Spencer looked at him from beneath her long lashes and gave him a slightly arch look.

"It wasn't *so* bad, Mr. Harcourt. Why, in fact, I think that I rather enjoyed it. It was certainly most... *salutary*, as your sister might say," Kate said, gently disengaging herself from his fervent grasp.

They walked a little way on.

"And did you... did you *like* what you saw of me in the Old Stables, Mr. Harcourt?" She wanted to ask him if he had found any of the other sights in the Old Stables to his liking, too, but her instincts were to leave this question for another time. Whatever he was, Robert seemed no prude, of that she was sure.

"Please, call me Robert. Yes, very much, Kate. I did, very much. Indeed, if the eyes can fall in love, mine have fallen head over heels with you."

"Sir... Robert... you flatter me." Now

Kate was enjoying her flirtation immensely. It appeared that she would soon have this handsome young man wrapped around her little finger. And what a perfect revenge on the treacherous Fordhams! "But I am puzzled as to why you did not take me when you had the chance, for so many others enjoyed me that day."

"Oh, I desired you, of course, but I could not bring myself to share you with those coarse yahoos... those boors!"

Kate looked down, surprised to see that he again was holding her hands. She looked up at him and suddenly he took her head in his hands and kissed her, long and hard. She felt a surge of exultant love and hope in her breast; she hardly knew this man, but already she sensed her motives for revenge evaporating; she could feel herself falling passionately in love with him.

"Oh *Robert*," she gasped, laughing with pleasure, when they broke the kiss in order to regain breath, "have you come to rescue me?"

By way of an answer, Robert kissed his damsel in distress once more, and she could feel his impressively large manhood press urgently against her thigh.

When they arrived at Walthrop, apart from the odd housemaid going about her duties, the place seemed almost deserted.

They went first to her room, which seemed to be just as she had left it, in order to leave her valise; then they repared to his. They looked at each other almost shyly as they stood in front of the large four-poster bed.

"Come, Mr. Harcourt," said Kate teasingly, "I see you need some encouragement."

She undid the top button of her dress.

* * *

Robert saw her face flushed and excited and heard her moaning and gasping as she engulfed his swollen cock in her mouth.

He watched contentedly. His cock felt wonderful in that hot, velvety mouth. She was as wildly aroused by their encounter as he; just as promiscuous and just as daring, he guessed, and he had never found anyone that could suck his long, thick cock as tenderly as she could.

He enjoyed the show, watching Kate with her hair still tied up in a neat bun, head bobbing up and down on his throbbing cock. He groaned deeply as he watched and felt the bulbous head of his prick encircled by her busy little tongue. The cherry-pink of her lips looked beautiful against the mauve-pink skin of his circumcised glans, and it felt heavenly.

Robert grasped her thigh and pulled it to his head. She was kneeling with her full, pale buttocks facing him. She raised her thigh as he pulled it toward him and straddled his head with her luscious hips, not missing a stroke on his cock as she did so.

Here was a delightful prospect for Robert – Kate's fragrant, hot fanny spread out invitingly right in front of his flushed face and hungry mouth. Her dark brown pubic hair was soft and fine, and it framed her plump, downy fanny-lips; above, by contrast, he noticed that her tightly puckered anus was quite devoid of any hair. He stared at the beautiful, juicy sight for a long moment before taking his first taste of her wet cunt.

Grasping the smooth, soft flesh of her buttocks, he spread her arse-cheeks and exposed even more of her lovely fanny. He saw her cunt open, her arsehole spread, and her swollen clitoris strain from between her turgid fanny-lips as he pressed his face into her steamy crotch.

Kate released an ecstatic groan as she felt Robert's skilled tongue touch her excited cunt. She sucked harder on the head of his cock, straining to get more of his massive prick into her mouth as he began to excite her juicy fanny.

Robert pressed his tongue lightly against Kate's exposed, pink little bean and licked smoothly up through the humid valley of her cunt, into her dripping hole, and on to her flexing arsehole – where he lingered for a moment to tantalize the wrinkled pucker. He then swept his tongue quickly back through the hot cleft of her cunt, pressing more firmly this time, and plucked the throbbing clitoris into his mouth, sucking hard.

"Aahh... that's right... suck me, suck my little nubbin, dearest Robert... suck it hard!" she cried, her mouth involuntarily leaving his cock as the delicious feelings in her loins swept through her entire lithe young body.

She sucked his cock back into her quivering mouth, pulling him in deeper this time as he continued to tease her clit. He quickly understood the way she liked it. He kept a steady pressure on that swollen bud of clit-flesh, feeling it throb and move, and then began to flick, lightly and maddeningly, with the tip of his tongue. Keeping the hot little love-button trapped with his lips, he vibrated it expertly with his tongue. He felt the warm sensation of his cock going deeper and deeper into her mouth in return.

"Mmmm...," she moaned, her mouth and the back of her throat stuffed with Robert's cock. She was going wild with lust. She wanted to devour his cock. Robert's hot mouth sucking and manipulating that most sensitive part of her cunt was unleashing all her passion.

With her animal desires blazing, she

fought back the reflex to gag and pressed her head down farther on Robert's long cock, letting it slide all the way into her clasping throat passage. Her lips pressed against his pubic hair as she gulped and sucked on his hot prick.

A gasp of delighted disbelief came from Robert now as he felt her throat consume his entire cock like a velvet-gloved hand. He let her throbbing clit escape from his sucking mouth and began again to lap his tongue through the entire hot, wet region of her loins. He licked in long strokes, massaging her burning crotch from her clitoris to her delicate little arsehole.

His actions were becoming more and more frenzied, and he could no longer pull his face away from her fanny to look at her erotic image in the long cheval looking glass at the end of the bed. He knew that as they each sucked and licked one another, their sexual bonds were becoming stronger and stronger, binding them together in a cocoon of love and lust.

Kate was close to spending. Robert could tell by the way his cock was deep in her throat, and by the way her hips were starting to buck and twitch above his face. He could also tell by the way her cunt-hole was squeezing his tongue as he plunged deep into her fanny, and by the way her arsehole was flexing excitedly.

He knew that now was the time to push her over the edge of bliss – before he came and while she was at the peak of her passion. He again captured her twitching clit between his lips and massaged and pulled firmly on her small pink bud. He felt the tiny centre of passion throb as he pulled, her hot fanny-flesh stretching and straining as he clamped down more firmly.

"Ahhh... uuhhh!" His skillful manipulation of her clit did the trick. Her head was raised above his cock, her face a mask of passion as she howled and moaned in the ecstasy of her orgasm.

As her spasms gradually faded, Kate relaxed her lust-tightened body. She hung her head back between Robert's legs and sucked gently just at the head of his bloated cock. She sucked with her eyes closed, a placid, satisfied expression on her sweet, pretty face.

Robert took one last, loving lick at her tightly flexed arsehole and gently pushed her hips forward. She knew just what he wanted her to do. All that was needed was a hint.

She crept forward slowly on her knees, still straddling Robert's body. He watched with pleasure the lovely scene her spread arse-cheeks made as they shifted from side to side, opening and closing to reveal her arsehole and the dark-haired pouch of her fanny-lips.

Robert thought back to what they had being doing only minutes before. The image so fixed in his mind was still that of Kate finger fucking, her actions feverish and tense. One hand was at her tits, kneading her soft, white tit-flesh and pulling at her erect nipples. Her other hand was still between her smooth thighs: her fingers alternately plucking at her clit, dipping into her twat, tantalizing her arsehole. Her face now had the expression of a woman totally absorbed in the wonderful task of bringing herself off. And doing a very good job of it.

But now Kate's hips were poised over Robert's cock – it waved erect, pointing straight at her luscious loins. Reaching between her legs, Kate spread her neat inner cunt-lips with her fingers. She pulled them widely apart, opening her twat for Robert's magnificent nine-inch prong. She slowly lowered herself until the head of his large tool was just touching the inner opening of her fanny. She released her hold on the flaps of her cunt and they surrounded the head of his cock with a warm wetness.

"Oh, dearest Kate, your fanny... it's burning my cock, it's as if..." Robert groaned as the head of his flesh-truncheon was engulfed by her warm fanny.

Kate placed a finger on his lips.

"Dear Robert, I know. It's as if we've been lovers forever. Now feel this," Kate said lustily. "If you think my fanny's hot on the outside, it's scalding on the inside!" She relaxed her hips and allowed herself to descend smoothly and steadily, his prick sliding straight into her cunt. Her hands went involuntarily to her smooth belly as she felt a wonderful sensation of fullness.

Robert's hot cock was a perfect fit in her tight fanny. She lowered her bottom until she was resting on Robert's pelvis, his cock buried to the hilt in the warm folds of her flesh.

"Ohh... that is so divine... now, can you feel how hot it is?" she asked in a hoarse, passion-filled voice as she enjoyed the tightly stuffed feeling in her deep fanny. She watched herself in the mirror at the foot of the bed. She had a full frontal view of her lovely body. Her long chestnut hair had escaped the bun and now fell down on her shoulders. Her tits were taut and uplifted with jutting pink nipples. Her slim waist tapered out to full hips with the soft patch of her dark pubic hair at the base of her belly pressing into the black hair that encircled the base of Robert's cock.

"Yes, my sweet," Robert answered. "It's boiling... it's boiling hot in there!" Robert was enjoying the wonderful tight heat of her fanny and admiring his double view of Kate at the same time. He looked down at his hips where she squatted with her flawless back and achingly beautiful arse facing toward him. He could see the base of his cock encircled by the turgid lips of her cunt, and her arsehole nestled against his pubic hair, as she held his cock all the way inside her fanny.

Turning his head slightly sideways, he was able to see her front side reflected in the long mirror at the foot of the bed. She was stroking her tits, lightly pinching her swollen nipples as she watched her reflection and relished the feeling of his big cock inside her loins. He could see his balls pulled tightly up against the base of his cock, directly under the triangle of her thick bush at the apex of her lower belly.

She raised her body smoothly and slowly. His cock appeared, inch by inch, sliding wetly out of her fanny. It looked angry and glistening from the heat and wetness of her cunt. The lips of her cunt adhered to the smooth skin of his cock as she raised her hips higher. Her cunt seemed to suck at the prick that stretched her inflamed, pink lips. She stopped at the point where only the head of his burning tool was enclosed in the moist folds of her fanny-flesh.

"Dearest? How does my... *cunt* feel?" Kate asked, thrilling at her use of the dirty word, knowing now how all men seemed to love that first complete immersion in her twat. She flexed the mouth of her cunt as she held her body steady, squeezing his yielding cock-head, the only part of his rock-solid member that was rubbery and pliant. Just as Molly had told her she should.

"Oh, dearest Kate, it is the prettiest, most accommodating, tightest cunt I have ever had the pleasure to fuck," Robert groaned, closing his eyes tightly from the biting sensation of her fanny squeezing his red, swollen cock-head. She's one in a million, he thought to himself. The only girl I've ever fucked who could control her fanny that way.

She began lowering herself again, her fanny sucking in his cock. He watched with pleasure as the huge head of his massive prick first stretched her fanny-lips to their widest point, then moved smoothly on through to her hot, tight cunt. He had been amazed at the ease with which she could consume his cock with her mouth or her cunt. Would her arse be able to take in the whole thing? Perhaps; but not as easily, and certainly not without some further coaxing from Robert. His cock was long and thick, and many of the women he had fucked just couldn't endure it. Not Kate, it would seem. He was thrilled by the way she was able to take in his gorgeous cock with her lips or twat.

She was halfway down his cock by now, feeling the big head plough through her cunt-hole. Her fanny-juices were beginning to flow. She could feel them dripping from her widely stretched slit. Her pubic hair and arsehole were becoming saturated with her sweet, sticky juice.

Kate sighed deeply as the mouth of her fanny touched his pubic hair. She immediately began to slide her fanny up his cock again. She sped up her movements and was soon beginning another hot downward stroke. She began to groan deep in her throat with each upward stroke, then suck her breath sharply as she moved swiftly back down Robert's silky-smooth cock. She could feel the firm but mercifully spongy cockhead touch her cervix. The feeling was a little disturbing, she thought, but satisfying all the same.

Robert watched her reflection once more in the mirror. Her face was flushed, her head thrown back with her mouth open, as she passionately stroked her tits and belly and thighs. At the downward portion of each thrust, she would grasp his fat balls in her hand and lightly squeeze his swollen scrotal sac.

As Robert looked back at the rear view of her body, her hips twitching and her buttocks parting with each stroke, he realized that he was near to shooting his spunk into her fanny. He knew that now was the time to slow down and prolong the pleasure. He also knew that she might just be aroused enough at this point to take his entire cock into her tight, sexy arsehole.

"Hold your horses, my lovely!" Robert commanded, grabbing Kate's arse tightly as he leaned forward. He held her there at the top of her stroke, her fanny barely making contact with the head of his cock.

"Let us slow the pace from canter to trot," he said softly, teasing her by flexing his cock in the mouth of her cunt.

"Oh, Robert!" she moaned, eyes half-closed in passionate, lusty need. "Give it to me... please give it to me now, dear one!"

Robert held on tightly to Kate's squirming arse and prevented her from ramming herself back down on his cock. He watched with delight as her tender arsehole flexed excitedly. He felt sure that she was hot enough to let him stuff his whole cock into that tight little hole.

"You shall, dearest, my sweet tormentor," Robert said in a voice thickened by lust. "I'll give it to you... in your arse."

"Oh, Robert," Kate moaned, "anywhere... wherever you wish!"

He looked on with pleasure as she raised her hips and released his cock from the strong grasp of her fanny. He was surprised at how easily she agreed to his demands. Most of his conquests usually had to be coaxed along for a while before they would let him stick that big cock of his into their arses.

He closed his eyes in delighted anticipation.

When he opened them again, he saw that she had leaned forward, raising her arse away from his cock. He loved to watch a girl prepare herself for getting fucked in the arse.

She spread her thighs wider. Reaching down between her legs, she began to dip her long fingers into her dripping cunt then rub the juices over her tightly flexed anus. She was first using only two, but she gradually worked three fingers into her still-excited fanny. Slowly withdrawing them, enjoying the feeling as she did so, she smeared her sweet, sticky cunt juices all over her pink-brown arsehole.

Robert enjoyed this almost as much as he knew he would love the feeling of her tight arsehole sliding down his cock. The thrill of watching a beautiful woman playing with her fanny and arsehole was almost beyond compare.

As she gradually soaked her puckered anus in love-juices, it seemed to take on the dark pink, feverish colour of her inflamed fanny-flesh. Once it was properly lubricated, she began to lightly probe into the opening with her fingertips. Slowly, she pushed two fingers into her hot opening, stretching it wider and wider. She continued to alternately plunge her fingers first into her arsehole then back to where the juice dribbled over the little stretch of her perineal skin, wetting her anus still more, finally sinking the coated fingers almost full-length into her tight, puckered opening.

Robert saw her passionate expression in the big mirror as she leaned toward it, her fine bosoms hanging forward and swaying with her movements.

Robert again returned his gaze to the real, flesh and blood Kate and saw that she now had three fingers sunk completely in the widely stretched hole between the cheeks of her perfect, white arse.

"Oh... Robert," she gasped feverishly. "I'm ready... I think... no... I'm *sure* that I'm ready for your cock."

"Wait, dearest one," Robert replied. "Move your lovely *derrière* back here for a minute and give me a taste of that sweet arsehole before I put my cock in there."

Kate complied with his order. She crawled backwards on her knees, her arse spread wide. Each backward movement she made with her knees pulled her pert buttocks apart invitingly as her loins moved closer to Robert's waiting mouth. She stopped with her beautiful arse and fanny spread wide and wet right in front of Robert's face.

"Oh, yes, you lovely girl," Robert moaned, placing his hands on the smooth arse-cheeks directly in front of him. He stretched them apart as wide as they would go, making her arsehole actually protrude slightly from the wet crevice between her arse-globes.

Pulling her towards his face, he opened his mouth and pressed his lips to her pink, puckered hole. He held his open mouth against her closed anus. He licked it lovingly and tickled the very centre of her tight little rosette with the tip of his tongue. He even liked the way her anus tasted and felt after she had been playing with it and rubbing it with her fanny-juice.

Once again, he pressed his tongue hard against the centre of her tight ring of arse-muscle. Her fingers had loosened her tight sphincter and his tongue slid easily into the hot passage. He fucked his tongue in and out of the squeezing hole, enjoying the thrilled little moans and gasps his actions caused Kate to make. He kept his lips pressed around the musky opening and continued to manipulate her anus with his tongue, just as if he were kissing her mouth.

Kate let a long, lusty sigh escape her throat as she felt Robert's tongue probe deeper and deeper into her inflamed anus. She felt him remove one of his hands from her buttocks and soon felt his experienced fingers

...ke hold of her swollen clit. Shivers shot deliciously through her body as her clit was tweaked and lightly pinched. Then she felt the simultaneous deep thrust of his tongue and an extreme, squeezing pressure on her protruding clit.

"Aahh... squeeze my little button... squeeze it, dear one!" she screamed. "*Ohh*, that is capital – so, so very good indeed... fuck your lovely tongue into my arse, my lover, my tender ravisher! Ohhh... oh... oh... I am spending... *spe-spending!*"

Robert loved the sound of her sexual excitement. He squeezed harder on her throbbing clit, sticking his tongue as deep into her anus as it could possibly go as a powerful orgasm swept through her lovely body.

Removing his tongue from her hole, he pushed her momentarily drained body forward. "And now, m'dear. Now for the real thing," he said lustily.

She moved back down toward his still-erect cock until her hips were positioned above his throbbing prick.

"All right, place it inside," he ordered in a husky voice. "Come on... get it in your arse!"

Kate prepared herself for the next ordeal. She grasped Robert's thick tool in her fist and guided the head of it to the mouth of her arse. Placing the tip there, she began to slowly but steadily rest the full weight of her hips on Robert's dick. Robert moaned as he felt the sensitive head of his cock contact the hot flesh of Kate's anus.

Kate felt the bulbous head of Robert's beautiful cock inexorably spread open the tight ring of muscle and gradually enter her anal passage. She bore down slightly and wiggled her hips to help ease it into her arse, loving every sensation of the hot cockhead intruding into her bowels.

In the glass, Robert could see the look of ecstatic bliss on Kate's face as his cock began to penetrate. He was able to watch his dick disappear into her beautiful arse and watch the lovely reflection of Kate's face and body, both at the same time.

As the head of Robert's cock passed on into her squeezing rectal passage, Kate threw her head back and howled at the burning sensation it created in her belly.

"Ahh... it feels so good, dearest," she groaned. "Ohh... I love it, I love it!"

She reached down and grabbed her arse-cheeks with both hands and spread them widely apart to help accommodate more of Robert's big cock. Robert watched the lovely view of Kate's arse opening wider and wider as his cock disappeared inch by inch through the tight portal to her rectal cave.

"Yes, dear one! Squeeze it in there!

Squeeze my cock into your tight arse," he almost sobbed, so powerfully acute and delightful were the sensations that he was receiving now. Her arse continued to suck in more and more of his hot cock-flesh. He was stretching her entire rectum with his magnificent prick.

"Oooh...I love it," she cooed, unable to hold off the feelings of deep orgasm that were beginning in her belly and travelling up her spine. Her hand involuntarily reached for her twitching clit and began to manipulate it feverishly. Her other hand went to her swollen nipples and pinched and pulled the hot, hard, red buds. She was entering a realm of sexual ecstasy: her clit was being rapidly stimulated; her nipples and tits were being stroked and caressed expertly; her arsehole was being filled with the hard, hot meat of Robert's nine-inch cock. The only thing she lacked was something for her fanny, she thought, hungrily.

Robert took intense sexual satisfaction in both the feeling and appearance of his long cock sinking into Kate's bottom, and he also noticed her beautifully passionate reflection in the tall cheval looking glass.

Reaching forward, he took Kate by the shoulders and gently but firmly pulled her backwards until she was reclining against him. He had even a better view now of his prick jammed into her hot arsehole. His own sphincter tightened in sympathy. The mirror showed him every detail of the humid, daring penetration.

Robert reached to the shelf at the head of the big bed and grasped the rubber dildo that might easily have been the 'Punisher's' twin. Positioning it between her legs and guiding himself by the reflection in the mirror, he placed the big head of the fake cock at the mouth of her gaping fanny. He slowly pushed the rubber prick into the wet folds of her fanny-flesh. As Kate cried out in her utter erotic satiety, thrillingly, Robert could feel the hard shape of the dildo through the thin layer of flesh that separated vagina and rectum.

"Ohhh...Robert, you are killing me, my sweet... but please, yes, do it to me... in my arse... in my cunt..." cried Kate, her voice rising two octaves, "ahhh, dear, sweet man, *f-fuck me... b-bugger me!*" She was at the very brink of orgasm, beginning her rapid ascent to ecstasy.

Robert watched their reflection: now both her hands were at her fine breasts, kneading and squeezing the large jiggling mounds of white flesh; her hips were bucking and writhing and sucking in the last few inches of his hot cock into her bottom; her head was thrown back with her long chestnut hair flying about; her pretty face was flushed and distorted by a rictus of sexual bliss.

He felt the hot jism rising within his loins. The bucking movement of Kate's arse was bringing him off without her even beginning to stroke his heavy cock. He pistoned his cock roughly, spasmodically, in and out of her arse, burying it completely in the tight, hot confines of her bottom.

"Uhhh... Robert... I'm spending, oh sweet Lord, I *s-sp-pend!*" Kate gasped frantically as the plethora of all her stimulations finally drove her over the brink into complete sexual frenzy. She squeezed and pressed her tits like a madwoman. Her loins twitched and bucked to gain each inch of penetration into her cunt and arse. She was spending beautifully, more fulfilled that ever before, her strong feelings of love for Robert supplying the satisfying emotional dimension that was so clearly lacking in the previous couplings she had enjoyed.

Robert felt himself coming, too. He felt the thick, hot jets of semen travel through his cock, spurting into the deep interior of Kate's arse.

Both their bodies shook and quaked as the intense powers of orgasm overcame them at the same time. They lunged feverishly against each other with all the force in their bodies... once... twice... three times... their orgasm took control. Their hot, flushed bodies

did a sexual dance, moving to the need of their sexual drives, stirring the deepest source of their physical lust.

Later, much later, after Robert had rung the bell and a flustered Mrs Beveridge herself had brought them a cold collation and a decanter of claret, after they had eaten and drunk and the afternoon sun cast long shadows on the carpet by the bed, they had made love again, more tenderly, less energetically perhaps, but no less intensely. As she climaxed, Kate threw her head back and wrapped her long, lithe legs around Robert's waist, pulling him deep into her.

Afterwards, they slept, rising only so that Kate could change in time for dinner.

Chapter Seven

The next morning found Kate and Robert in their separate beds, slumbering late after a night of unbridled, passionate lovemaking; for whilst most adventures of the flesh were tolerated, and, indeed, on some occasions positively encouraged, by the Fordhams, a veneer of respectability had to be maintained for the benefit of the staff who were not aware of the true Walthrop morality.

In the conservatory, her preferred location

for discussions of a serious nature, Alice Fordham was discussing with her husband this unexpected romantic union of her brother and the new governess.

"It *shall* not be!"

Sir Bradley looked mildly alarmed. He had seldom seen his wife so annoyed.

Alice Fordham's eyes were flashing with rage. When her younger brother had taken her aside and announced his love for Kate, she had appeared to greet the news of this romance with remarkable equanimity, however under this façade she seethed with anger. Her own, darling brother! With that little slut of a governess! Besides, she wanted young Kate Spencer as her *own* plaything. It was a disaster – her brother was hotheaded enough to *marry* the little baggage. But she would never be accepted into polite society, a common schoolmaster's daughter! Alice knew that she must keep this last reason as her trump – for her other two motives were less easy to defend.

"And so, my dear, what shall you do?"

"What shall I do? Why, I'll make the scales fall from my beloved Robert's eyes... I'll make him see her for the depraved, dissolute little slut that she is..."

A plan began to form in her mind, and slowly her smile turned into a vicious smirk, transforming her anxious, angry expression into one of malicious cunning.

* * *

Kate was uneasy. Robert's unexpected departure after lunch – on an urgent matter of business that requested his presence in London – had left her, once more, feeling vulnerable and exposed. Intuitively, she knew that Alice Fordham disapproved of her liaison with Robert. It was time to be diplomatic, to be discreet. And above all do nothing to irk her mistress or master. Perhaps in this way she could bring Alice to take a more sympathetic view of the romance with her brother. Accordingly she immersed herself in her duties as governess: Ellie's tutelage had been sorely neglected in the past few days. However Alice, too, seemed to go out of her way to be pleasant and avoid any reference to Kate's experience at the Old Stables.

It was for that reason that, two days later, Kate was surprised to receive another invitation to the Hall of Worship: that evening there was to be a meeting of the Followers 'and a few of our oldest friends'. Alice stressed that she was under no obligation to come, and if she did, she could attend merely as an observer. So Kate accepted, albeit not without a few qualms. It might have seemed churlish not to.

After dinner that evening, Ellie, Alice and Kate set off for the Hall of Worship. Ellie was in a state of high excitement, and even during the short carriage ride she was unable to sit still, her thighs rubbing against each other in a state of nervous arousal. The girl was addicted to sex, thought Kate.

The lanky Reverend Pike and his button-eyed wife were at the door to welcome the Walthrop party, Bella Pike as effusive as ever. As usual, the Hall was ablaze with the light of a hundred candles, their golden light playing over the naked bodies of the Handmaidens and the half-dozen or so Followers some of whom had, rather to Kate's dismay, already disrobed. Alice handed her a glass of red wine.

"Kate, my dear, I know you will be taking a back seat in tonight's revels, for you are no doubt keeping yourself for my brother. And so you should! But I am so happy that you have agreed to join our fun tonight, if only as an observer. After all, you are nearly one of the family now!"

Kate thought that she could detect a certain tightness in Alice's voice that made her wonder about the older woman's sincerity. But she decided to let it pass. Surely there was no harm in being here, in watching. It might be fun, and besides, she could chat to some of her new friends from the Old Stables. She took a comfortable seat at the back of the hall and looked on, slowly sipping her wine.

* * *

How could it have happened?

Kate found herself as naked as the rest of the company! She stood, noticing that her clothes were lying on the pew beside her, neatly folded in the way that she would normally leave them. Had she undressed herself, she wondered vaguely? If so, she could not remember doing so.

The Handmaidens were busy.

There was Molly, servicing a plump woman in the *soixante-neuf* position, their buxom bodies beautifully matched. There were Susan, Meg and Annie attending to various gentlemen and ladies that she had never seen before. There was Irish Bess rising and falling in the lap of none other than Vincent Barchester, and there was sloe-eyed Ruth, servicing another matronly Follower, as the slim, pretty girl knelt between the woman's widely splayed thighs, her head bobbing up and down.

And there was little Ellie... dear God, she was being buggered by the Reverend Pike! And she looks as if she is loving every second, thought Kate, as she watched her pupil thrust her pert bottom back at the randy old goat.

She heard groans and squawks of pleasure behind her and turning saw that Bella Pike was on all fours and gratefully accepting the hard thrusts of Alice Cordham as she knelt behind and rammed the Punisher into the scrawny woman's tight quim by hand. The obsequious pastor's wife quivered with delight.

Looking over Bella's head, Alice's eyes met those of her employee. She raised an eyebrow as if to say, 'are *you* ready for me now?'

Kate nodded. She was. Every nerve in her body called out for sexual release, for sensual pleasure, every square inch of her body wanted to be caressed and stroked, squeezed and licked. Her mouth opened and closed, her tongue traced a sensuous path around the inside of her lips. Oh, she was ready... ready to love.

Her employer cast Bella Pike aside as a spoilt child would an old, used toy. She moved over to Kate. Once more, Kate was able to see how beautiful she was: a fine figure of a woman clothed, Alice Fordham was positively beautiful in the nude. Well, almost nude. She still wore her boots and stockings, tied with red garters. Her figure was voluptuous without being in the least bit plump, every single curve and every declivity was positively luscious to the eye. Her large breasts were still up-thrust and firm and her dark nipples exquisitely prominent and well defined. A deep, concave navel sat in the gentle swell of her belly and below that grew a dense bush of the blackest, softest hair that Kate had ever seen.

When Alice lightly pinched the sensitive tips of Kate's breasts, she almost climaxed there and then. She let out a deep, shuddering *'Ohhhh!'*

Alice Fordham continued to stroke Kate's beautifully shaped tits and her pointed nipples lovingly, fantasizing over the things she could have Kate do to her and the things she could do to Kate. Ellie came over to join them. Kate kept on thinking of the passionate picture they made for Ellie as Alice felt her young body, while the older woman contemplated just what she would instruct her keyed up young governess to do.

Alice remembered the way she had seduced her governess, had commanded her to do such excitingly humiliating things before, whilst under the influence of laudanum – and whilst not.

She knew that Kate was primed. So well primed, indeed, she reckoned that the young governess would do anything that she was told to do. An idea suddenly came to her: it was time to make her lazy daughter sing for her supper.

"Ellie!" she called sharply.

"Yes, Mother?"

"Come and lick your pretty governess's cunt!"

"Oh *Mother!*" Ellie reproached her, "must you always use those vulgar words?"

Lady Fordham merely grinned wolfishly at her daughter and, pushing Kate into a supine position onto her back, pointed to the junction of Kate's thighs, and uttered one word.

"*Lick!*"

Ellie was already between Kate's legs and had hungrily glued her wide-open mouth to her pink, needy cunt, as if to devour her. Within seconds, the Fordham governess was bucking and writhing, her mouth uttering little moans of intense pleasure, under the intense and skilled cunnilingus that her virtuoso pupil gave. While her daughter took care of her at one end, Alice squatted at the other, lowering herself gingerly onto Kate's upturned face. Kate had no choice but to kiss and tongue the deliciously musky wet flesh and swallow the outpouring of sex juices that issued from the woman's aroused vulva. The realisation that she was acting as a sort of incestuous bridge between mother and daughter had not escaped her and she derived an illicit thrill at the thought. Alice shuddered briefly with a small preliminary orgasm and then slowly got to her feet from her squatting position. She substituted her own fingers for Kate's mouth and started to gently frig herself, knowing exactly where this action would lead: faster and faster she strummed her red, engorged clitoris as she groaned and bucked in ecstasy: then she uttered a sharp cry and, quivering from head to foot, squirted a powerful jet of clear liquid that splashed onto Kate's face and chest, covering her breasts and belly.

"Oh, *Mama!*" murmured Ellie in awe.

"That will suffice now, Ellie. You may stay to watch us now, if you wish," said her mother dismissively, as she removed her boots and stockings. Another idea had formulated. She knelt and started to feel Kate's sex. Ellie sat close by on the floor, her knees drawn up to her chin, her eyes wide as saucers. Alice withdrew her hand from Kate's soft, hairy fanny and inserted three fingers into her own gaping cunt. She stroked the wet flesh lightly, stirring up her hot juices, drenching her fingers in her hot liquids. "Did you know that Ellie and I ate all of Lord Barchester's spunk?" she asked Kate in a low, salacious voice. "No, I don't think you saw us... you seemed to be far away in your own little world. Never mind. Have you come to appreciate a woman's juices?"

"Oh, yes... let me taste yours, Alice... let

me taste your fanny," Kate begged.

"Here," Alice responded, presenting her juice-drenched fingers to Kate. "Lick my juices off my fingers," she instructed.

Kate complied, licking at Alice's wet hand, clutching it, running her tongue over every finger then sucking each one of them into her mouth. "Mmm... you taste so good," she gasped between licks. Alice pulled her hand away again and returned it to her big, meaty, gash, soaking it again in her juices and enjoying Kate's hungry stare as she did so.

"Oh, Alice, please let me lick your lovely fanny... let me taste... let me kiss it," Kate begged.

"Just do what I tell you," Alice commanded gently but firmly, "then I'll let you lick my cunt." She pulled her wet, sticky fingers out of her hole and angled her hips up higher so that Kate had a complete view of her spread crotch. She pushed her fingers into her arsehole, closing her eyes and gasping from the powerful feeling as she slowly kneaded them in and out of the tight hole.

"I'll let you lick my arsehole, too," she said lustfully, watching Kate's entranced gaze as she stretched her anus in ever-widening circles with her wet fingers. Once again, Kate was struck by the incongruity of Alice Fordham's use of these highly vulgar words. But at the same time, they acquired a delicious wickedness when they were delivered from her aristocratic lips in her perfectly enunciated, upper-class tones.

"Taste them again, sweet one," she instructed as she pulled out her finger and once more held them invitingly in front of Kate's face. Kate was even more passionate this time in her licking and sucking of Alice's wet fingers. She devoured every drop of Alice's juices, inflamed by the combined taste of Alice's sweet and musky arsehole and fanny.

Alice reached now for Kate's fanny and buried two of her slim fingers in the tight, young opening. Kate moaned loudly as Alice stroked the hole rapidly, stimulating her flow of juices. Withdrawing her fingers, she spread Kate's slippery exudate over the large, erect nipple of one of her own magnificent tits. Cupping the juicy tit in her hands, she held it toward Kate's mouth.

"Lick my nipple," she instructed, her voice quivering with lust. "Taste your own fanny ... taste it ... suck it!"

Kate eagerly obeyed, mouthing Alice's sharp nipple hungrily, noisily sucking her own sweet juices from Alice's tit.

"Aaaaaaahhhhhh... that's good... suck it, dearest, suck it!" Alice gazed lovingly at Kate's fresh, innocent face, flushed with excitement at the taste of her own love juices and Alice's fat nipple.

Alice pulled her foot up level with Kate's open slit and began to rub and caress the swollen, wet lips with her smooth, sensitive toes. Kate sighed deeply, leaning back against the couch. She grasped Alice's warm foot in her hands and rubbed her toes harder against her aching fanny-flesh.

"Stick my toes in your cunny," Alice gasped, loving the feeling of warm, slippery little lips against her tender foot. "Fuck yourself with my toes!" Holding Alice's foot with both hands, Kate began to probe into her cunt-hole with Alice's big toe, stroking it in and out of her hot slit feverishly. Kate moaned with pleasure at the penetration into her fanny, and Alice felt the warm, wetness of her juices enclose her the tip of her foot.

"Now in your arse... fuck your arsehole," Alice ordered, watching with delight as Kate obeyed. She felt Kate's tight arsehole open easily as her big toe pressed against its puckered opening. She was amazed and excited by the ease with which the rosy pink hole accepted the penetration. She panted with lust as she watched Kate jerk her arse-cheeks back and forth shamelessly, luxuriating in the feeling.

"Suck my toes... lick them... lick your juices," she commanded breathlessly, pulling her toe from Kate's tight arsehole and moving her foot towards her mouth. If Kate found this request repugnant in any way, she showed no signs of it. She lapped and slurped hungrily at Alice's lovely toes, sucking them into her mouth and tantalizing them with her tongue, hungrily licking and devouring her own juices. "Oh... you are perfect, quite perfect," she sighed as Kate continued with her sucking. "Now you may suck my fanny. Put your head between my legs," she ordered, "but keep your bottom up here by me." She guided Kate's head to her crotch and positioned her so that her head was pointing downward between Alice's thighs and her knees rested beside Alice, her arse high in the air and spread wide open to Alice's touch.

"Just take my button, my clitoris, between your lips," she said hoarsely, her voice thick and breathless with lust. She felt Kate's hot mouth encircle her clit, sending shivers through her loins. "That's right... just hold it with your lips... flick it... flick it with your tongue!" she cried as Kate's hot, quick tongue lambasted Alice's unusually large clitoris, sending shivers of delight throughout her entire body.

Savouring the exquisite sensation of her clit trapped and throbbing in Kate's mouth, Alice turned to Kate's lovely arse beside her. She spread the smooth young cheeks even wider with her hands and gazed greedily at the lovely sight. Kate's soft brown pubic hair covered the fat pouch of her youthful fanny. The inner labia protruded slightly from the downy outer folds of flesh, her clit peaking out from its little hood, red and swollen. Clear, syrupy love-juice oozed from the pink flesh at the mouth of her cunt, musky and enticing. Her arsehole was a delicate, pinkish tan in colour and tightly puckered, tightening and slackening, just waiting to be licked.

"Keep flicking it like that... uuummmmm... that's right, dear girl," Alice moaned as she continued to relish the sensation of her governess's mouth tantalizing her clit. She began to play teasingly with Kate's fanny. She ran her fingertip along the edge of the slick inner lips, then pressed her finger between them and stroked it up and down through the oozing groove of her cunt. She poked the mouth of Kate's vaginal opening provocatively with her fingertip, eliciting deep, muffled groans from Kate. She plunged her fingers deep into the hot, fleshy hole, feeling the way the strong muscles of the young girl's hungry vagina sucked her fingers inside and gripped them tightly. Stroking and stretching the soft folds of fanny-flesh for a few moments, she withdrew and gently plucked at Kate's throbbing clit, stroking it the way she would stroke her own. As Kate's groans increased with each new move Alice's fingers made, her arse began to jerk greedily, wanting more and more stimulation. Kate began to remove her mouth from Alice's clit.

"Keep sucking!" Alice commanded, enjoying her power to control Kate and to have her hold her clit so excitingly in her mouth. She continued to tease Kate's fanny as she luxuriated in the feeling of her clit throbbing and warm inside Kate's mouth, being caressed by her lips and lightly flicked with her hot tongue. Diverting her attention from Kate's clit, Alice turned her consideration to Kate's wrinkled arsehole as it now flexed with hunger and excitement. She plunged her fingers deep into the hot opening, once more amazed at the way it stretched almost as easily as did her cunt-hole. She fucked her fingers in and out rapidly before finally giving in to her desire to suck and lick Kate's luscious pink cunt-flesh.

She pulled Kate's thigh across herself, straddling Kate's spread arse-cheeks over her tits. With a lusty sigh, she began to devour the sweet young flesh with voracious lips and tongue. Pulling her smooth buttocks closer, her movements became wilder and more passionate as Kate began to stroke her own tongue up and down through Alice's dripping, voracious maw. Their actions became more and more frenzied as each girl drove the other to higher peaks of lust and animal desire. Alice felt herself being completely overwhelmed by the tremendous current of sexual power that ebbed and flowed between them. Their moans became sharp gasps of pleasure and ecstasy as their mutual sucking and licking took on a fevered pace. Their bodies bucked and writhed against each other in total abandon as their pleasure peaked and then began to slowly subside. And playing shamelessly with herself, young Ellie had watched it all...

Chapter Eight

Robert Harcourt read the cryptic note again. The housekeeper, Mrs Beveridge, had handed it to him on a salver the moment he had returned from his business in London.

It was in his sister's hand and read simply: 'We are at the Hall. Join us if you wish to discover your *inamorata's* true nature.' Just as he was about to leave, Mrs Beveridge coughed discreetly.

"If I may make so bold, Mr Robert, there is something I think you ought to see..."

She led him to the pantry and pointed silently to a bottle of laudanum and a half-empty wine bottle. Robert looked at her in mute enquiry.

"That poor girl. I can tell you nothing more, Sir. It is more than my job is worth…"

Robert cut the woman short with hasty muttered thanks and, with a face of thunder, turned on his heel and left.

* * *

For a long time after their mutual climax, Alice held Kate in her arms. Then she leant up on one elbow and looked down at the confused young girl with cold eyes.

"Listen to me you sweet little hussy… you belong to me. And you will never, *ever*, ensnare my brother with any of your cunning little wiles, your cheap, tawdry sentiments, or by playing the put-upon, innocent young miss; no, you may banish any ideas you may have entertained of being the next Mrs Harcourt. You are a common little trollop, good for nothing more than ridding your betters of their baser passions. My brother has had his fill of you, you would do well to forget him now, or it will be the worse for you." She paused to squeeze one of Kate's breasts painfully, as if to gain her attention, "Do you understand, you silly little wanton?"

Kate nodded dumbly, the tears stinging her eyes, not for the first time feeling utterly betrayed and alone. How could Robert have left her after all that had passed between them? The passion, the caresses, the tenderness, the protestations of love?

"Give me some more wine, will you please?" was all she could bring herself to say. Alice Harcourt smiled and beckoned to Ellie to refresh Kate's glass from the little decanter that she had brought with them from Walthrop.

Kate gratefully gulped down the contents, rejoicing in the warm, comforting glow that it brought to her senses. She dashed her tears away with the back of her hand. She would show them all! She cared not for love or any such romantic foolishness! She needed sex! That was her basic requirement... that was all that she needed from anyone.

She looked around her. What she saw would make any Roman orgy look tame. All over the Hall's interior men and women were indulging in every sexual congress that she had ever thought possible. The Handmaidens were busier than ever, but now Molly came over to them.

"Come, Kate, his Lordship has a fine stand – as hard as nails – and he is calling for you!"

Kate allowed herself to be led by the hand to a dark alcove where Lord Barchester was reclining on a sofa. Ruth was kneeling to one side of him and teasing his balls with her mouth; his erection was superb – quite perpendicular – and Kate's mouth watered involuntarily. She wanted it! She needed it!

Molly and Ruth, their pale and dark complexions contrasting prettily, helped her astride the recumbent peer, Ruth's agile fingers directing the head of his cock into the groove of Kate's cunt, while Molly parted her pretty buttocks to reveal her neat arsehole. Kate could feel the slight yield of his spongy cockhead as it found the entrance to her vagina. She pushed down hard. Whimpering with pleasure she accepted the full length of his hard shaft into her tight quim.

Vincent Barchester gasped as he felt the hidden fingers of Kate's cunt muscles massage his erection. He moaned in delight as she began to rise and fall upon his cock like a horsewoman astride a trotting horse.

Unfortunately for Kate, at that very moment, the tall, stooping figure of Edgar Pike hove into view. For a while he watched the little group. Then, striding over to them, he grabbed Molly by the scruff of her neck and forced her down onto his large but drooping penis. Molly went at her task like a trooper. She took the pastor's phallus into her mouth and started to suck. Soon the Reverend Pike's cock was hard again. As Molly did her best to continue to lick and fondle his cock and balls, he knelt behind Kate and clasped her hips, arresting her up and down motion. With a hand on each arsecheek, he drew them apart to reveal her little brown anal pucker.

"Come, Ruth," he commanded, "prepare the way for me!"

The slight girl ducked under his arms and started to use a skilful tongue on Kate's arsehole.

Kate bucked and writhed at the intimate contact, but tried to keep still, if only for the girl's sake. She felt Ruth's tongue flatten and cover the sensitive surface in a broad swipe, then dance delicately over its little striations, then stiffen and point, drilling the tight sphincter as if wanting to gain access to her very bowels. Lord Barchester looked over Kate's shoulder and grinned approvingly at the activity behind her.

"Are you intending to take Miss Spencer in the manner of the Sodomites, Reverend?"

Pike gave him a horsey grin.

"Why yes, my Lord. I believe I am!"

"Then please, Sir, do not hold back on my account!"

Kate's mind reeled with the implication. They were going to take her both at once! She was to be no more than the meat between two bits of bread! A sandwich! Her arsehole twitched nervously against Ruth's industrious tongue. Please, no, dear God! Not that! She recalled the Reverend's huge size, and her eyes watered at the memory. She looked behind her, straight into the implacable, lust-distorted features of the bogus parson.

"*Nooooo!*" she cried.

It was too much. Kate struggled to get up. But she had not reckoned with Lord Barchester's strong arms that tightened around her waist like a vice, completely immobilising her. Molly bent down and stroked her neck as one might soothe a pet animal, trying to comfort her.

"There, Kate, don't take on so... you will enjoy it, to be sure..."

The words were hardly reassuring as Pike's enormous cock once more started to batter at the cringing little sphincter between Kate's trembling arsecheeks.

"Please, Reverend, I beg you..." cried Kate craning her neck to appeal to the man.

But she could see that he was implacable, his face a mask of lust, and nothing would deter him from his goal. Indeed, to Pike it seemed that her buttocks were jutting towards him and obscenely, gently rotating as if in invitation. Her thighs tensed and rippled in lithe strength as she shifted on her feet, and then Lord Barchester reached around her back with his hands and tenderly pulled apart her buttocks with his fingers, disclosing, in an even more obscene gesture, that little dark hole for the parson's pleasure.

Kate's tiny revealed anus, which now appeared so raw and vulnerable, was as a bullseye in a target to Pike, and her bottom rotated as if on its own axis, taunting and teasing the man so intent on once more plundering the depths of her rectum, and who had begun to manipulate his rigid cock, pushing its spongy, yielding head until it lodged just inside her anal ring.

Kate moaned piteously as her double-impalement began to take effect. It was as though two great wooden stakes were running her through, so tight and full were the thrustings she now endured. "Aaaaaaggggghhhhh!" she groaned with each inch that she forced up into her tight, hot passage. Oh God, I'm being punished! I'm punishing myself! Yes, yes! Beautiful, painful, sweet agony! This is for Robert, for betraying him... Her confused mind screamed these muddled thoughts at her as she waggled her buttocks and skewered back upon the huge prick burrowing its relentless, never ending length right up into her wide-stretched rectum. There! It's home! All the way! I can feel the pubic hair of his pelvis against my crotch. I've taken it all right into my arsehole and its magnificent head is in my bowels! Oh mercy! It is so horribly wonderful...!

And then, sensing through the thin wall of flesh separating them that Pike's mighty truncheon was fully inserted into Kate's backside, Barchester started to heave and thrust until, between them, they built up a sort of ghastly rhythm. Kate screamed in lust and pain... but the pain is receding, she thought... and the lust is advancing. Surely I am, as Alice Fordham says, nothing but a little whore...

And as this thought entered her head, Alice swam into her view. Now she was wearing the thick black Punisher around her loins, erect and menacing. She smiled at Kate.

"When Pike has finished with you, I will take his place," she whispered hotly in Kate's ear, "but he'll be a while yet. He likes to take his pleasures slowly."

As Alice wandered off to find another group, Kate reached between her legs and with difficulty placed her hand over the tight, sperm bloated scrotums of both men, caressing them, squeezing them to see if she could not hurry the process. For while she no longer found them painful, she derived no pleasure from their actions. Her delicate fingers were joined by Molly's and Ruth's. Soon the men were overwhelmed by the squeezings, ticklings and probings of the three girls' fingers. Molly pulled the Reverend's muscular buttocks apart until Ruth and she were greeted by the sight of his hair-encircled, brown anus; while she held them thus, Ruth ducked her head down and the pretty, slim girl trailed a saliva-moistened tongue along the cord-like ridge between his wide-spread hair-lined buttocks. Then she gave him the same treatment as she had to Kate, tauntingly circling the puckered brown hole, painting his inner ass-cheeks with her saliva, finally stiffening her tongue as its tip endeavoured to penetrate the crinkled sphincter of his rectum. This proved too much for the man and he gave a soft groan of pleasure and discharged the contents of his heavy balls into the depths of Kate's battered rectal passage.

When Alice returned, there was no sign of the Reverend or Ruth and Molly. Kate, however, seemed to have gained a second wind, for she was riding Vincent Barchester with such energy and enthusiasm that even Alice was impressed by her stamina. She waited for her chance and when Kate flopped down onto the chest of her lover, she quickly thrust the bulbous end of the grooved rubber dildo into the reddened, sperm-leaking little hole between the girl's bottom cheeks. It slipped in easily and Alice gave a little crow of satisfaction as she pushed in all the way until her bushy mound slapped against the out-thrust buttocks of her governess.

And then, she froze in a moment of horrible recognition.

For the face of Kate's lover was now only inches from her own and she saw clearly in the dim light that it was not that of her old friend Vincent Barchester: her own brother's features stared at her, his look menacing, one quizzical eyebrow slightly raised as if to ask, yes, Sister? What is it that you want of us?

Alice gave a great cry of shock and fell back... covered in confusion. Her own, darling brother... she could not believe how badly her whole mistimed ploy had backfired.

Later she learned that far from catching Kate writhing in passion between two debauched men, Robert had come across her weeping, being consoled by her two Handmaiden friends. She had flown into his arms; she had begged his forgiveness for doubting him, and for thinking that he might ever desert her... He had looked lovingly into her eyes, his anger rising as he saw how the opiate she had unwittingly consumed had reduced her pupils to pinpoints. Shedding his clothes, consumed by passion, he had possessed her once more, while she wept with joy and shuddered with the most intense pleasure, her arms encircling his neck as if she meant never to let him go again.

Envoi

Kate laced her arm through Robert's. They looked out of the carriage window as the train drew out of Windsor Station. Her heart swelled – they were travelling to London to start a thrilling new life together – and at last she could look forward to some sort of sustainable contentment, if not happiness. She realised that some might regard their union as imperfect and lacking in any real substance – immoral, even; there was no talk of marriage, but then Kate did not wish there to be. In the last few weeks – no, in the last few *days* – she had become most pragmatic about affairs of the heart and flesh. Her matrimonial ambitions had, accordingly, faded somewhat. She and Robert had discussed their future together in this new, down-to-earth spirit. Marriage was something that might come with children, but there was no desire to procreate on either of their parts. She was to be his mistress, his 'kept woman', and she was more than content with that status, despite its limitations.

She watched the Berkshire countryside drift by and her mind was carried back to Walthrop, the Old Stables and the Hall of Worship. How unimportant all that seemed now! She had made an uncomfortable sort of peace with Alice: Robert had forced his sister to destroy the contracts that Kate had signed. The Fordhams had been contrite. They had promised to mend their ways and, at Kate's insistence, had also given their word that they would treat the Handmaidens especially well, ensuring that they were well placed once they 'retired' from 'active service'. And Ellie – sweet, dim little Ellie. How she had wept at Kate's departure! And the Handmaidens, too: why, when she went to the Old Stables to take her leave, there had not been a dry eye in the place, except that was, for young, pretty, sloe-eyed Ruth. She had whispered in her ear, "Take me as your lady's maid to London – you will need one and I am good with dresses, my dear parents trained me well!" Kate had thought for the briefest of moments, then she had asked Robert if he was agreeable. He was. And thus it was that, seated opposite them, Kate's very first lady's maid sat demurely, reading an improving book. And Kate, who could only guess how useful it might be to have a lady's maid who was 'good with dresses', certainly knew how useful it was to have a Handmaiden who could lick fanny divinely.

To be continued...

Just a few of our many titles for sale...

Los Angeles Girl & Punishment for Claudia
Special double edition. Model and virgin, Della, finds herself giving more than she wants to on her photo-shoots in *Los Angeles Girl*. Claudia is a Nazi spy in wartime USA with a penchant for spanking, being spanked and submissive sex in *Punishment for Claudia*.
£12.50

Backdoor Virgins
After catching her husband with his flame-haired mistress, beautiful heiress Ellen Fielding is determined to seek revenge. Embarking on a nymphomatic spree of epic proportions, she not only loses her anal virginity but plans an erotic retribution for the two lovers that they will never forget.
£7.50

Nicole's Pregnant Hunger
On returning from her honeymoon, Nicole Ashby is delighted to learn she is pregnant. And pregnancy proves to be no obstacle to her insatiable lust either. But who could the father be? Not only is her husband in the running, but most of the men in his predatory family too.
£7.50

Ranchers' Dirty Wives
When Danny McCluskie brings his gorgeous, virginal, young bride Billy Jo to his family's cattle ranch in Texas, the scene is set for marital bliss. Until Danny has a riding fall and is laid up for a month. Enter three horny brother-in-laws, a megalomaniac ranch manager and others determined to seduce her.
£9.50

Turkish Delight
After being cruelly raped by her callous husband on her honeymoon, Lucy Dean finds herself adrift in one of the most exciting and dangerous cities in the world: Istanbul. Drugged and abducted, she faces a life of sexual slavery, but first she must be taught the tricks of the trade.
£7.50

Orderline: 0800 026 25 24
Email: eps@leadline.co.uk
Post: EPS, 54 New Street, Worcester WR1 2DL

EPS

WWW.EROTICPRINTS.ORG